MW00891626

My Mr. Manny

a novel

JENNIFER GARCIA

ISBN: 1517463424
ISBN-13: 978-1517463427

DEDICATION

To all my family for giving me fun, crazy, and great memories to spark new stories. To my husband and children for always supporting me in all my endeavors. I'm the luckiest woman alive!

CONTENTS

Prologue	Hide and Seek	1
1	Kick the Can	2
2	Simon Says	4
3	Man Hunt	7
4	Mother May I	11
5	Dodge Ball	17
6	Hopscotch	21
7	Red Rover, Red Rover	25
8	Miss Mary Mack	29
9	Duck, Duck, Goose	33
10	Telephone	37
11	Pin the Tail on the Donkey	43
12	Double Dutch	47
13	Musical Chairs	51
14	Four Square	57
15	Catch and Kiss	61
16	Ring Around the Rosy	65
17	Chopsticks	70
18	Follow the Leader	75
19	Tiddlywinks	79
20	Marbles	84

21	Knucklebones	88
22	Pick-up Sticks	94
23	Tag, You're It	98
24	K-I-S-S-I-N-G	102
25	Pitching Pennies	107
26	Tic-Tac-Toe	112
27	Stone Skipping	117
28	I Spy	122
29	Peek-a-Boo	128

ACKNOWLEDGMENTS

Thank you to all those that assisted me in the creation of this story. It takes a village and I'm thankful to have been supported by an amazing one. I couldn't have done this without the encouragement from my friend, Lisa Bilbrey. Support from R.E. Hargrave, M.B. Feeney, and Lorenz Font. Elizabeth Lawrence worked her editing magic on the first edition, which remain in the second edition. The second edition cover was designed by Murphy Rae at Indie Solutions.

Prologue
Hide and Seek

My heart raced, and my breaths came in short pants while I stood against Mrs. Lawson's house. I did not want to be found, so I pressed my small hands flat against my chest to hold back the fear and excitement.

While I calmed myself against the gray, vinyl siding, I paid attention to my surroundings. The scent of lilac and jasmine was overpowering in the heavy, hot air. There was no breeze from the nearby ocean, thus no relief from the heat wave.

Over the sounds of my neighbor's blaring television, I heard my cousin, Lori, scream at the top of her lungs. They'd caught her. The laughter that followed was too close for comfort. Alex was "it," and I'd have to stand my ground until he moved further away.

When I didn't hear anything else, I looked around the corner of the house to see if anyone was near me. My heart beat in my chest, and the fear of Alex sneaking up on me had me on edge. The coast was clear. I bolted, ducking under apple trees and jumping over jasmine bushes through the back yards of all my neighbors.

The houses in the neighborhood were tall, and the yards were massive, lending us little coverage. I hopped over a low chain-link gate that separated one yard from the next. Few of the properties had fences, and those that did had only low barriers that were small enough for us to jump.

It was dusk and almost time for us to go in for the night. The streetlights weren't on yet, so I assumed we had a few more minutes. When I reached the last house to my goal, I peeked my head out from the side of Mrs. Andriotti's house to scan the street. I had to get across to the other side and touch the light post in front of my house without getting caught. A few kids were there already, but Alex was nowhere to be seen. I hoped he was searching for me somewhere else and not hiding near the post. First looking left then right, I booked it as fast as I could. Everyone started screaming, but I touched the post just before someone grabbed me. Even though I knew who it was, I jumped.

"I'm safe!" I screamed.

"You're so lucky. I almost had you," Alex complained with a pout.

Gasping, I tried to catch my breath, but my laughter made it difficult. "Ha ha! I made it. I guess you're gonna have to try harder to get me next time," I teased.

"Mia, it's time to come in," my mother yelled.

The smile on my face faded in an instant, and I waved to everyone before I turned around and went inside.

Chapter 1
Kick the Can

I shook my head with a smile. Nights like those had been so carefree and fun. I had been about eight years old then, and when I thought of those times on our street, I remembered the feeling of owning it. Trident Avenue was a small street right off the beach in Winthrop, Massachusetts. Our house, yellow like a beautiful buttercup flower, was set almost in the middle of the street. The green, expansive yard was outlined with a three-foot chain-link fence. We had an apple tree, a grape vine, and a volleyball court in our yard. We could have fit an Olympic size swimming pool and still had room left over, but my mother, Christine, would never have gone for that. The smell of lilacs and fresh grapes had wafted through the air all summer long.

Next door lived a sweet boy with Down syndrome, Guy. The other kids teased him, but I always stood near the fence to speak with him while he paced up and down. I seldom understood what he said, but that didn't matter — he was alone, and that was something I understood well.

My mother didn't worry about me being kidnapped. My cousins and I could run the street, and the neighbors didn't complain if we passed through their yards. The long, thick, black asphalt was our playground. We were safe on our street. Times were simpler.

Life changed so much that I forgot those fond memories of things that were once important to me. Days playing hide and seek with the kids on my street were a product of the time I came from.

I stayed on Trident Avenue until the end of my sophomore year. All six of my cousins lived next to me growing up. I didn't have any siblings of my own, so they became my pseudo-siblings. I was picked on a lot because I was different: different because I was an only child, because I didn't have my father there, and because I didn't look like them. On top of that, I yearned for friendships but put up walls at the same time. It was like a "love me/stay away from me" type of thing. My cousins were from a family of six siblings, and if I had a falling out with one of them, they all ended up mad at me. I just never fit in. Instead I guarded myself and never got too close.

My dad left when I was three because the marriage between him and my mother didn't work out. He and I had been very close before he left. Stories of the time before he left my mother always consisted of him taking me all sorts of places. We would hang out, just the two of us. After he left, I heard that he was traveling, living for short times in Colombia and Mexico but finally settling in California. I was the kid who was never home during school vacation because I was visiting my dad in San Francisco or Los Angeles — wherever he lived at the time. My cousins, as well as the other kids, were able to bond with each other during vacations. I never had that chance, because I was always gone.

Alex Greco was one of our neighbors who always hung out with my cousin Vitto. They were a year older than me. Vitto was a genius and spoke of attending MIT. His sister, Loretta — Lori for short — had dreamed of moving to New York or California to attend a fashion design school. My other four cousins were much younger and were in grammar school or junior high. Everyone had plans and was moving on, but I still had no idea what I wanted to do with my life.

Chapter 2
Simon Says

My dad had been pestering me for years to live with him in California, but it wasn't until the end of my sophomore year that I decided to go. Dad wanted a better life for me, one he thought I wouldn't get in small town Boston. Going to Culver City High School in California was an experience in and of itself; the mix of people was amazing. Not needing to look like my cousins so I could fit in, I wasn't the odd man out anymore. Being an only child with divorced parents made me different in our small town in Boston. However, in Los Angeles, I fit in and gained confidence in who I was. It was my chance to find myself and become a stronger, more outgoing person. Or so I tried.

Even though I loved living in Southern California, I still missed my Boston home and wished I could have had my extended family, my mother, and pseudo-siblings with me to experience this new life. I went back home to visit my mom as much as I could and always squeezed in a visit with my aunts, uncles, and cousins while I was there. The longer I remained in California, however, the more what my dad had told me when I moved made sense: even if I went back, my old life would no longer be mine. The longer I stayed away, the less I belonged in Boston. In the end, I gave in to my new life and let the old one go.

I also missed the seasons. In Boston, autumn was the most beautiful time of year. The leaves would turn all the colors in the crayon box. As kids, my cousins and I would collect bags full of them and use them in school for arts and crafts. The air during that time was crisp, but not cold. The humidity of the summer was gone, and we could breathe again before the biting cold arrived.

Being a California resident for two years afforded me the ability to attend the University of Southern California. With the small scholarship I was awarded and the resident pricing, it allowed me to attend the expensive school. My dad helped with some of the tuition, and I took out a loan for the rest. While attending USC, my roommate, Susan, wrangled me into going to all the football games. During my first game, I was quick to find out football was very important at USC. Our closest rival, University of California Los Angeles, played against us.

That very first game, the Trojans entered the field in their cardinal red and gold, and as I scanned our side of the bleachers, all I saw was Trojan color. People were everywhere, packed in next to each other, yelling and screaming. The air smelled like hotdogs, popcorn, and beer. Spectators walked up and down the bleachers with trays of food and drinks in their hands, getting settled before the game started.

Susan had dressed me up in a Trojan's jersey and had painted my face—so embarrassing! I didn't like big displays, but Susan was more rowdy and much more outgoing than me.

On the other side of the field, the bleachers were filled to the sky with true blue and gold, the colors of the UCLA Bruins.

At halftime, Susan had dragged me to the bathroom. The bleachers cleared quickly, and everyone walked around in different directions on the walkways. People pushed and shoved from all sides, smashing us like sardines. I hated crowds, which gave random people the chance to grope you without consequence. I had always been very particular about my personal space. With all of the unsolicited touches to my body, I was losing my patience. It was imperative for me to get out of that crowd and fast; otherwise, I might have lashed out and thrown down with someone for pushing me. The crowd was so thick that I felt the blond hair from the girl in front of me tickling my face. I felt so relieved when we made it to the bathroom. Then, we had to stand in line. It just seemed like a lot of work. The crowds, lines, and the fact I still wanted to get something to drink, which meant another line.

"What is wrong with you?" Susan asked. My head snapped up, and I shrugged. She had been working overtime to get me out of our dorm room and into the social scene more. Susan was beautiful, with a full curvy body, freckles, bright red hair, and blue eyes that reminded me of a crystal blue ocean.

"I'm not a happy camper. I can't stand all these people touching me. I'm on the verge of an anxiety attack," I said with a nervous chuckle. I was serious, but Susan's expression made me laugh. She just scrunched her face in disbelief. I knew I was annoying her and felt bad, but she should have just let me stay in our room.

"Mia, I understand your idea of fun is hanging out at home, but you have to get out once in a while. We only get to do college once," she said in disbelief at my disinterest in partying.

"How long is halftime, anyway?"

Susan just laughed at me and pulled me forward in line. "Come on; it's almost our turn." There were two girls in front of Susan, and I was about to pee my pants. While I was shifting from foot to foot, I focused again on how much I hated people. All at once, three stalls opened and a girl popped out of each of them, happy and giggling. I shook my head again because I just didn't understand what was so fun about this whole night.

Susan and I began our journey to the snack stand, where tons of people were standing around talking and ordering. After I received my order, Susan and I began walking back to the bleachers when I heard someone call my name.

I turned around but didn't recognize anyone. Then, I saw a guy walking toward me.

His blue eyes and big dimples looked familiar, but I couldn't place him, so I just stood there like an idiot waiting for him to reach me and say something.

"Hey, I was hoping that was you," the mystery guy said.

I looked around to make sure there was no one else behind me.

"Um, you were talking to me, right?" I questioned pointing to myself.

He smirked and said, "Mia Balducci, right? It's me, Alex Greco. You know, from Trident Avenue?"

"Oh, my God, Alex! What are you doing here?"

I didn't know what came over me, but I gave him an awkward hug since my hands were full. He smelled of soap and cologne, an older brand that no one used anymore but that still smelled good on him.

I stepped back to introduce Susan to Alex, but she wasn't next to me any longer.

"Tonight, I'm here supporting my buddies on the field, and I'm a sophomore, business major."

"Wow, so you followed your dream to go to USC? That's great, Alex. It's great to see you."

A group of guys with their hands full of beer, popcorn, and hotdogs from the bar were standing a bit behind Alex, laughing and looking our way. A big guy called out to him, and Alex held up his index finger to let him know he'd be right there.

"Hey, I've got to get back to my friends, but can I call you?"

I nodded my head, gave Alex my phone number, and walked back to my seat on the bleachers.

Alex had grown up to be a very handsome man. He was of average height, around five-eight, with light brown hair and those same baby blue eyes I remembered so well. He was a part of home that I missed: the people, the warmth, and the familiar. His smile warmed me from the inside out, and I knew it had to be showing in my own smile. It was so nice to have a piece of home here in this unfamiliar place.

Chapter 3
Man Hunt

Alex called me a few days after that football game.

Our first date was at Paco's Tacos, my favorite restaurant, which served the best Mexican food ever. Located on a very busy side street on the outside edge of Culver City, Paco's Tacos wrapped around the street corner and into the adjoining row of businesses.

The waiting area had a big sofa that wrapped around three of the walls and a table in the middle. On the ceiling, paper bandanas hung in colors coinciding with the closest holiday. Mexican Independence Day had just passed, so the bandanas were red, white, and green. A Mexican woman stood in the corner, rolling dough for homemade tortillas and cooking them on a big round griddle. The smell of fresh flour tortillas made my mouth water.

Two big fish tanks sat in the middle of the dining room, surrounded by round tables. Beautiful, brightly-colored fish swam along a tank floor piled with aqua rocks, coral, and floating plants.

The bar at the far end of the restaurant was well stocked, and I was ready for a drink. I decided on an icy-cold mango margarita, and Alex ordered a beer from the bar. They were the perfect drinks to go with the delectable food we ordered: my favorite plate, carne asada tampiqueña, and Alex's combination plate with a chile relleno and a steak taco.

A smile spread across my face in pure happiness while I looked at Alex sitting in a place I loved. It felt so good to have the comfort and memories of my past connect to my present. He looked so handsome, his blue eyes sparkling in the light from the fish tank and his cheeks flushed from the alcohol.

When he reached across the table for my hand, I felt the softness of his fingers. They were not the hands of a person who did much physical labor; they felt too soft and supple.

Alex and I caught up on what we had been doing for the past two years. I told him about my last two years of high school, and he told me about becoming a sophomore at USC and promised me I would love college.

We talked about our plans after college and both agreed we would not be going back home to live — ever. I had fallen in love with California over the past two years, and so had he.

ço ço ço ço

When I became a sophomore, Alex and I moved in together. We rented a condominium in Culver City about seven miles away from school. The condo happened to be in the same gated community where I'd lived when I went to high school. The community was split: townhomes on one side and condos on the other. My dad lived on the townhouse side.

The land was the old MGM lot where The Wizard of Oz had been filmed. The gated community had a huge man-made lake. A beautiful recreation building sat at the water's edge. Inside the building were a party room and a gym. The lake was long and lined with olive trees. Ducks floated on the water and bathed near the fountains that peaked out of the water. You would have thought you were in an exotic place somewhere far from the busy city, but on the other side of the big block walls, the traffic and craziness was all still there. It was a beautiful property, secure and guarded.

Alex's and my lives meshed well, and it felt good to be loved at last. I hadn't dated much in high school, even though all my friends had been boys. Girls were too catty for me, and between my big mouth and my shyness, most girls never knew what to make of me. It seemed as if I was always searching for love and friendship, but I never found it until Alex came back into my life. Comfort came in the piece of Boston that Alex gave me. When I looked at him, it made me feel like I was still in touch with the good memories from home.

෧෧ළළ

School was a priority, and it kept me busy. Before I knew it I only had one more year of college to go and wasn't sure what I wanted to do after that. Alex graduated, and without a lot of fanfare, he went straight to work. His father lined up a job for him through a business connection with a big company in Century City, and it was a great starting position with a hefty salary. He worked hard and long hours since he was new and still learning. He had to prove himself.

My senior year was tough, but I knew with my full attention I could finish. I often felt tired and emotional, which at first I thought was due to being run down. After a few months, however, I found out I was pregnant. I was so afraid Alex would be upset when I told him; instead, he was happy and said it was the best Christmas present he had ever received. Somehow, I made it through school, pregnant and exhausted, but the accomplishment made it worth it. When I graduated in May, our parents were there to celebrate with Alex and me. I was six months pregnant and feeling oversized. I still had three more months to go and knew by the end I would be huge.

My mother was there for my graduation, and it was the first time she had visited me in California since I had lived here. I always went to visit her because she said it was "easier" and that I could visit my family. I had always agreed, but it was nice to have her in the place I now called home.

Alex and I sat next to one another during the graduation dinner, with our parents surrounding us on all sides.

"Your aunt hasn't been feeling well lately, and her kids are driving her crazy. She's always calling me to complain, and I tell her in all seriousness that I don't want to hear it," my mother said, and then she sighed. My mother was a tall woman with a round face who, even in her late fifties, had flawless, cream-colored skin. I had her natural hair color, which was a russet brown. Since going grey, she had been reduced to dyeing it, but it was nearly impossible to tell. I wished I had her soft-looking skin, though.

I loved my mother so much, but she had a tendency to talk about nonsense. She was the type that would stop and tell a complete stranger her life story. On one of my visits back home, we drove to Rockport, a small coastal town with quaint shops, to go window-shopping and see the sights. We found a great store that sold magnets in an array of designs. I broke off to browse, and when I found my mother, she was talking to a store employee. For no less than forty-five minutes, she told story after story of her life. The lady was much too polite to say anything or interrupt her, not that she had a chance; my mother didn't even break to breathe. I saved her by purchasing a couple of magnets and ushering my mother out of the store. Now here she was, talking my ear off.

"God, Mia, and then she starts to complain about my brother and how he never helps her with those kids because he's always working. But the truth is he's home every night in time for dinner, and then goes over their homework and stuff. I just think she's a chronic complainer—"

The dinging sound of the silverware against a glass brought us out of our conversation. I was relieved. If my mother didn't want to listen to my aunt telling her all that nonsense, I didn't know what made her think *I* wanted to hear it.

Clink Clink. Clink.

"Can I have your attention, please?" To my right Alex stood, clinking his glass with a big smile on his face. When he was sure he had everyone's attention, he pushed his chair back and got down on one knee and turned to me.

"Mia, I am so happy with you and so thankful that we ran into each other at that football game. I can't imagine spending my life with anyone else. Will you marry me?"

I was in shock. I hadn't expected a proposal, but the more I thought about it, the more I realized it was perfect. My hands were crisscrossed over my chest, and my breathing was heavy. I had tears streaming down my cheeks, contradicting the big smile on my face. Looking down, I saw Alex's hands were holding a small, open red box with a beautiful solitaire diamond ring. It was gorgeous.

My mother cleared her throat to snap me out of my stupor. I looked up and noticed Alex's smile began to falter, and I realized he was waiting for my answer.

"Yes, yes I'll marry you!"

Alex's face smoothed, and the smile became genuine again. He plucked the ring out of the box and placed it on my finger.

The whole restaurant burst into applause, and the staff began singing a congratulatory song in Italian. I looked around at my loved ones and then at Alex. I could do it; I could be a wife and a mother. It all seemed so easy. Little did I know this was a decision that would plague me for years to come.

Alex and I decided that since the baby was coming soon and we wanted to be married before then, it would be wise to take advantage of having everyone in town already. We applied for our marriage license immediately, and after the two-day waiting period, we got married in the courthouse with our parents as witnesses. I had never thought about getting married before and didn't care much about what type of wedding I would have. As far as I was concerned, it wasn't about the wedding itself; it was more about the couple connecting.

A huge celebratory dinner followed at Paco's Tacos. I invited Susan, and Alex invited a few of his closest buddies from school. It was a nice evening and great to have all of our friends and family with us.

After dinner, Alex's mother squeezed me tight and whispered in my ear, "Mia, I'm so glad my boy found you all the way over here. A nice Italian girl from the neighborhood." I hugged her back and thanked her. "You call us when that baby comes, okay?"

"We will, Mrs. Greco." I gave her one last hug before she stepped back so her husband could hug me goodbye. They were all going home, and I was sad. Everyone had to get back to work and on with their lives.

My mother spoke next. "Honey, now you call me if you need anything. I want to know when my grand baby comes, and I'll try and make it out here to help. It depends on what my schedule is at the time. But you know I'll try," my mother said.

As she was boarding the plane with Alex's parents, she was still shouting things out to me. I was so used to it that I almost didn't get embarrassed anymore, but Alex's ears were bright red. Well, it was time for him to get used to his new mother-in-law.

Chapter 4
Mother May I

Our beautiful little girl was born on the tenth of August, two weeks late. She was perfection with her long nose, pink, full lips, and head full of russet-colored hair. She was the spitting image of me, save the crystal blue eyes. Lucia Grace, the light of my life, weighed in at seven pounds, eight ounces, and was twenty-one inches long. When I held her in my arms for the first time, I knew I had someone to love me back forever — someone who would need me and never leave me. I knew in that moment that the unconditional love between a mother and a child could never be broken. She was my whole heart and soul from that day forward.

I called my mother as soon as she was born, because she wasn't able to be there. She was so excited for us and begged us to take tons of pictures for her. My dad sat proudly in the waiting room for his turn to hold his granddaughter. It was strange watching my dad hold her, and it made me wonder if he had held me like that when I was a baby. Did he look at me with the same pride he had when he looked at her? And if so, then why had it been so easy for him to leave me? I knew I would never ask those questions and didn't want to ruin the moment with my self-pitying thoughts. Instead, I took many pictures of my baby girl with my dad and with my one true friend, Susan. I knew I would cherish those memories forever and have them to share with my baby girl when she was old enough.

Life moved in a flash after Lucia's arrival. Dirty diapers, midnight feedings, rocking her in the chair, and watching her sleep occupied my time. I hadn't noticed at first, but Alex continued to work long hours even after the baby was born. It didn't matter to me at the time because I was lucky enough to stay home with our baby.

When she turned three years old, Lucia was able to enter pre-school. I wanted to work while she was in school; I needed to get out in the job market before I was considered useless and too old.

I was lucky enough to find a job at American Airlines as the administrative assistant to the station manager of LAX, Los Angeles International Airport. I loved my job, and my boss was very flexible and understanding with my hours. He never gave me trouble, even when I had to leave to pick up Lucia from school activities, or when I had to deal with her colds and flus.

⧞⧞⧞⧞⧞

It was September, and my baby girl had just started kindergarten. When I looked in the mirror, I noticed my light russet hair had a few grays, and my honey brown eyes were starting to look sunken in. My face was haggard, with dark circles and bags under my lower lids, although my fair olive skin still looked supple. I knew I was still semi-young; I had just turned twenty-eight in April. I just wondered if my appearance was starting to reflect my age and exhaustion.

Things had been rough for us, and our family unit had changed so much. The caring and attentive Alex from the beginning of our relationship was no longer present, physically or emotionally. He continued to work as if it was the only thing important in life. His routine was to wake up in the wee hours of the morning and come home well after Lucia was in bed. I convinced myself he did it for us, so we could live in comfort, but I began to wake from my five-year baby fog and realize that I was happy without him. I thought about trying to change our situation and encourage him to spend more time with Lucia and me. It was sad how the past five years had flown by and how Lucia barely knew her daddy.

At the beginning of November, I decided I would wait up for Alex to come home. I wasn't quite sure what time he got home on a regular basis because I was always asleep before he arrived. I took a shower and shaved, then lathered myself in lotion and put on a sexy nightgown. It was lingerie, and it was prettier than the sweatpants and too-big T-shirts I sometimes wore to bed. I must have dozed off while waiting for Alex, but I woke up when I heard the shower running. Glancing at the clock, I saw it was twenty minutes past midnight. I wondered for a moment if that was the time he came home every night, which led to the thought of how odd it was for a CEO to be working that late every single day. I felt insecure about my decision to wait for him; it had been a long time. I thought about his reaction to finding me awake and waiting for him.

He walked out of the bathroom, flipping the light switch before he crawled into bed. I smelled the musk from his body wash and some mint from his shampoo when he climbed in next to me. He was on his side, facing away from me, so I scooted closer and wrapped my arm around him. Alex jumped as soon as my arm rested on his body.

"Hi," I said, for lack of anything better to say

He rolled toward me slightly and replied, "You're awake?"

"Yeah, I was waiting for you. I wanted to surprise you."

"Surprise me?" he questioned, with doubt and sarcasm in his voice. He was trying to be hurtful, and it was working.

Beginning to regret this whole idea, I realized I should have just left things the way they were; it would have been easier than putting myself out there just to get stomped all over.

"Well, I thought it was a good idea. I thought we could, you know, spend some time together."

"Mia, I'm tired. I just want to sleep. Maybe another time."

"Fine. Sorry to bother you."

What in the world? He wanted to schedule sex with his wife? This was what my life had come to.

A few hours later, I awoke to the sun shining through the window. As the first part of my morning routine, I slid my hand across the spot next to me on the bed, and as always, the sheets felt empty and cold. I felt stupid and vulnerable after what I had done the night before. After I'd gathered my courage and taken a chance to connect with my husband again, I'd been rejected. It left me cold, empty, and very hurt. I supposed it was my own fault for not doing it sooner, for allowing things to change between my husband and me, and for not trying to keep our marriage alive. I had heard from watching those daytime talk shows that sex was the first thing to go in a relationship, and when it did, it meant the couple was in a bad place. I had also heard that the hardest thing to do was to get the passion back and that restarting intimacy was a very difficult thing to accomplish, but if the relationship was important and worth saving, it should be done. Most women thrived on the emotional part of the relationship, and most men thrived on the sexual part. If either one felt slighted, they would look somewhere else for satisfaction. I thought perhaps I had fulfilled my emotional needs by loving my daughter with all my heart. With who and how did he fulfill his part? Because it wasn't with me.

I flipped the sheets back and walked into the bathroom. The beige tile was cold, so I hopped to the big, dark, red mat in front of the shower. I turned the knobs to let the water heat up and proceeded to get undressed. My favorite room in the house was next to the water closet. My walk-in closet was grand; it displayed all of my shoes and purses and had ample space to hang all of my clothes. Alex's was on the other side of the toilet and was the same size. This feature was what had persuaded us to rent this condominium, and now it was all ours. The owners had sold it to us a year ago, and I was so happy I wouldn't have to worry about moving or finding a new place that suited us.

I showered and got dressed in a knee-length black skirt and a turquoise silk blouse. The skirt showed off my narrow waist and the curve of my round hips. I did my hair and makeup and put on my jewelry before I woke Lucia.

She needed a lot of coaxing to wake up, so I sat on the edge of her bed and ran my hand over her hair and whispered to her. I made up cute little songs to rouse her from slumber.

"Lucia, Lucia, it's time to get up. Lucia, Lucia, you have to get ready for school. Lucia, Lucia, don't be a fool," I sang, and she giggled. She lay there with her eyes closed and stretched a bit. She knew that once her eyes were open, it would be time to begin her daily routine. I sang on and on until she graced me with eyes that glimmered like the ocean in the morning sun. It always made her happy — and what a wonderful way to start the day.

Lucia put on her school uniform, which was a navy blue plaid with thin white, yellow, and green stripes, a white blouse with a round collar, and a navy blue sweater. She wore navy blue knee-highs and black Mary Janes.

"Come on, baby girl. What do you want for breakfast today?" I asked.

"Good morning, Momma. Um . . . I think I want waffles today," she replied.

I made some coffee, poured her some orange juice, and popped the waffles in the toaster. She sat at the breakfast bar on the big stool and waited for her food.

"So, do you know what you're doing in school today?"

Her mouth spread into a big smile that showed the adorable dimples she had gotten from her father.

"Yup, we're working on our sight words today. I already know them all, but the teacher said I have to work on them with the class anyway."

"That's great, baby. You practice so much, don't you?" I asked.

"I do, Momma, and it helps me learn them faster," she said with such pride.

I placed in front of her a plate of waffles with very little butter and syrup spread on top, and I continued to sip my coffee.

My daughter was beautiful. She had long, russet brown hair with a slight curl, and her dad's crystal blue eyes. Her skin was fair, but in the summer, she tanned with ease and never burned. She was small and petite like a little flower. She was a girly girl who loved dresses and pink. In that aspect, she was nothing like me; I was more of a tomboy.

I drove Lucia to St. Augustine's Catholic School and walked her to her line. All of the children were split by classroom and had to line up until school started. It kept them all in order. We waited there until the teacher came for them. Lucia gave me a big hug, and her little arms could almost make it around my waist. I whispered, "I love you," in her ear when I bent down, and she kissed my cheek and whispered the same.

Lucia was my sunshine, my partner in crime, and my distraction. She was my heart.

After drop-off, I made my way toward Pershing Drive, our employee parking lot behind LAX. School began at eight for Lucia, so I had plenty of time to make it to work before I started an hour later.

I found a parking spot near the employee bus stop and snagged it fast. I was lucky; most days, those spots were full, and I had to park a long way from the stop. The busses ran every fifteen minutes and I always made the half past tram.

On the way to my workspace, I waved to some of my coworkers. Opening the door to my office, I heard my boss on the phone. I peaked in to let him know I had arrived. He nodded and continued with his conversation. Once I put my stuff away, I got down to business. Since my boss was the manager of a department with over three hundred employees, I was kept busy responding to their needs. I gathered their timecards from my inbox and began to work on payroll. Mr. White handed me some letters to type for him, and then gave me some money to pick up lunch for the both of us.

He said, "I'll buy if you fly."

I couldn't refuse because I was starving, so I ran to the food court and ordered us some sandwiches from Chili's.

Five o'clock arrived before I knew it, and while I sat on the bus to go to the parking lot, I decided to call Alex. I was hoping he would be home for dinner today.

"Hello."

"Hi, honey. How are you?" I asked.

"I'm busy." He sighed like he was irritated.

"Oh, I was hoping you could make it home for dinner today. I'm on my way to get Lucia from after school care."

"Mia, I can't. Being the CEO of this company is not easy. I have idiots working here, and I have to fix their mistakes. Paperwork never ends, and we are doing some employee replacements," he spat out. I flinched and scowled at his reaction to my simple request.

"I'll be home late. Don't wait up," he said.

I sighed. I was sick of his attitude and disregard for his family.

"That's fine, Alex. Lucia and I will have dinner alone as usual. It's not like we know any different. You work seven days a week and never find time for us," I whisper-yelled. There were a few other people on the bus, and I didn't want them to hear my conversation.

"Look, Mia, this is not the time to get into this. I gotta go, okay?"

"Well, it's never the time, is it? Do I need to make an appointment to speak with you, since you're never home for us to have any sort of conversation? You're gone before I wake up, and you come home after I'm asleep. This isn't normal, Alex," I huffed.

I could feel the blood rushing to my head in anger. My limbs began to tingle, and my nasty temper was signaling that I had sat back long enough. I knew I shouldn't have let this build up so long, but I had tried to remember he wanted the best for us. He was a dedicated employee; I just wished he was as dedicated to Lucia and me as he was to his job.

"Mia, I gotta go. This is ridiculous. I'm doing this for us. I have invested a lot of time here, and I know it will pay off one day."

"Bye, Alex," I said, my voice laced with venom, and hung up. I didn't even want to hear him say goodbye. I was so angry I didn't want to hear him at all.

I picked up my precious girl from school, turning my angry tingles into gooey happiness. Lucia was so excited to see me, and my chest felt tight with pride and guilt. I wished she knew what fun with her dad felt like. Who knew if she'd ever have the chance to experience that? I had no idea, and it scared me.

My arms wrapped around her in a hug and I smothered her face with kisses.

"Hi, baby girl. I missed you today."

She giggled from the kisses and said, "I missed you too, Momma."

When we got home, she sat at the bar on her stool and started on her homework while I cooked dinner.

Our galley-style kitchen was spacious, and the breakfast bar backed up to the living room. The whole condominium had an open floor plan, so you could see the dining room, living room, and kitchen all at once.

I breaded and fried some chicken cutlets, sautéed some spinach with garlic, and made garlic mashed potatoes. When dinner was finished cooking, I set the table for two, and Lucia and I sat down to eat. Lucia told me about her day and seemed interested in what I did at work while she was at school learning.

After dinner, I cleaned up the table, and then helped Lucia pack up her school stuff for the following day. Bath time came next. Lucia soaked in the tub and played with her toys while I washed her up and rinsed her off when her skin pruned

It was my turn to pick out the book to read to her, which I did while she put on her pajamas. She jumped on the bed, and I tucked her in and lay next to her while I read *Tallulah's Solo*. Lucia's head was on my chest, and my arm was wrapped around her. I loved being with her like this, but it always saddened me that her dad was never here to read to her or tuck her in.

That was how our weekdays passed. Every day, one after the other.

Chapter 5
Dodge Ball

One weekend afternoon, Susan, Lucia, and I spent the day at the Getty Center to look at their newest exhibition. Lucia participated in the kid's crafts while Susan and I examined the artwork, and then we three ate lunch at the museum restaurant.

While we ate, we hardly spoke a word, and the silence allowed crazy thoughts to run through my mind. The most wild idea popped into my head, and I whispered to Susan to see if she was available that evening. She agreed to sit with Lucia while I brought dinner to surprise my husband at work. This was not going to be a sexy-surprise. Instead, I was going to confront him and tell him that if things continued on the way they were going, we might not last much longer as a family. I did everything on my own anyway, so being an official single mom wouldn't be much different for me.

After we arrived home from the museum, I made dinner and entertained Lucia with Susan. The food was packed and ready to bring to Alex. I kissed Lucia and thanked Susan for staying.

"Oh, please, girl. I love spending time with her, and you have business to take care of. Go!" She laughed and pushed me out the door.

"Okay, okay. Thanks, Susan. Bye, Lucia. Love you," I yelled from the hallway outside my door.

∞∞∞∞

I pulled up to the valet in front of the Century Plaza Towers in Century City. The buildings were impressive, each with forty-four floors. Their triangular shape jutted high into the skyline, and their reflective windows made the buildings look like sparkling water in the sky.

The company Alex worked for took up four floors, with Alex's office on the thirtieth. I rode the elevator all the way up and made my way to his office. It was seven o'clock, and there were only a few lights still on. The receptionists' desks were all empty, and when I walked to the back of the expansive space to Alex's door, I saw light coming from underneath. His assistant's desk was cleaned up for the night, but there was a sweater hanging over the back of her chair and a purse on her workspace.

I knocked on the door. When no one answered, I walked in. His office was quite grand. Straight ahead was a dark mahogany desk. Behind the desk was a big bookshelf in black wood and mahogany molding with books, small statues and figurines, white decorative bottles, and a few pictures in silver frames. To the left of the bookshelf was a door that blended with the mahogany molding and could not be seen easily, but it led to his private bathroom.

There were plants on the floor, placed in the corners of the office, and two chrome chairs sat in front of the desk. To the right was a wall of windows that looked out into the courtyard of the towers. To the left was a black coffee table with four black leather club chairs surrounding it.

Beyond the sitting area were glass doors that led to his conference room, which was filled with a long mahogany table and black leather chairs.

The sound of a vacuum droned in the distance, and the smell of lemon Pledge filled the air, evidence of the evening cleaners.

I didn't see him in the office or sitting area, so I walked to the bathroom door, which was opened a crack. When I approached, I heard voices, so I stood as quiet as I could to hear what was going on inside.

I heard a woman crying.

I placed the bag of food down on the floor and stood at the crack of the door, peeking in. Alex had the woman in his arms. Her highlighted blond hair covered the parts of her face not planted in my husband's chest. Her hands were grabbing fistfuls of his shirt while she sobbed and sobbed.

He whispered that it would be all right, and she cried that she was tired of being the other woman and wanted him all to herself. I stiffened and felt heat rushing up my body all the way to my head.

Through her sobs, she cried, "It's been three years, Alex. All you have done is promise me you would leave her. You're never home, and you never see her, so why do you hang on?"

The soft hands that used to caress me were soothing her, rubbing circles on her back.

"Sshh, it's okay, Amber. I promise I will speak to her soon. You're right; I haven't been much of a husband to her in years. It's been just you for so long. You don't deserve this," he cooed.

She hiccupped, and my blood rushed like lava through my veins. My limbs trembled and tingled, yet I couldn't walk away from what I had just seen and heard.

I pulled the door open all the way, and Alex's head popped up in shock. When he saw me, his eyebrows almost touched his hairline. His blue eyes were bulging, and he released the girl immediately.

When she turned around, I got a better look at her. She was about an inch or two taller than me and had gray eyes. She looked young, but I couldn't be sure. Her figure was fuller than mine, and her chest was huge.

"Honey, wh-what are you doing here?" His voice was high-pitched and revealed his nervousness.

My hands were in tight fists, my arms stiff. While I stalked my husband, the girl backed away, still facing me. I wanted to hit Alex him for lying to me, for deceiving me, and most of all, for neglecting his little girl as he had been for years.

"Don't play me, you jerk! I heard everything I needed to know. Here I was, thinking you were working hard for us, instead you were here working on this ... this ... whore!" I screamed.

The girl paled, and her eyes went wide. She cried even louder, and it made me crazy. She didn't have the right to cry. She was involved in this mess. I spun around to address her.

"What the hell are you crying for? You're about to get everything you wanted. I hope you're proud of yourself for breaking up a family and taking him away from us. His daughter doesn't even know him, and he sleeps in the same house as her."

Alex, still standing next to Amber, had paled considerably. Sweat dripped from his hair to his ears — from nerves, I assumed. He swayed and looked unsteady, and I watched him brace himself against the wall, trying to keep from passing out.

"I'll pack up your shit and leave it outside the house tomorrow. Don't bother coming home . . . *ever!*" My face contorted in disgust. "I'll find an attorney, and you can have the divorce you've wanted so you can start a new life with *her*," I spat out the last few words, and I jerked my chin in her direction.

"Thank God your daughter doesn't know you exist. At least it won't be difficult to explain why you don't live with us anymore." With that, I turned around and walked out with my head held high.

"Mia, Mia! Wait!" he yelled, running after me. "Look, it's not as if you've cared these past five years. You acted like I didn't exist!" he yelled some more.

"You should have just asked me for a divorce years ago. It's not like I would have missed you." I told him as I kept walking, shaking my head in disbelief. "It all makes sense now."

I pushed the button for the elevator incessantly, hoping my action would make it come faster. Thirty fucking floors I had to wait.

Alex was approaching me, and I just wanted to be gone. In all honesty, I didn't feel hurt, just betrayed and angry. I hated lies and deceit. If I had known all those years that he was spending his time with another woman, I would have let him go. Why would I want to be married to someone who didn't want me?

The ding of the elevator alerted me to its arrival. I jumped in and pushed the button to close the door over and over. When the doors closed and I was alone, I knew I was safe from seeing him again — for tonight, anyway.

While I drove home, my mind was weighed down with thoughts of the future. What would we do with the condo? Would Alex want shared custody of Lucia? Would he move in with that husband-thief? Too many questions I wasn't sure I wanted the answer to.

When I walked into the house, Susan was on the sofa reading quietly. It was late, so Lucia was already asleep. Susan looked up when she heard me enter and, by the expression on her face, she knew something was wrong.

"That was quick. What happened?" she asked.

I squinted my eyes and shook my head. Putting my stuff down on the bar, I walked over to the sofa.

Susan slid her book onto the coffee table and turned to face me.

"What happened? Tell me."

"Oh, Susan," I breathed. Then it hit me like a ton of bricks, and I broke down for the first time since I'd left his office.

"I got there, and he was consoling some woman in his bathroom." I wiped my tear-filled eyes with the heel of my hand, and Susan paled and sat back, stunned and silent.

"The short of it is: they're together, and I'm in the way," I said.

"What?" Susan stood up with her hands fisted and her face bright red with anger. "Why aren't you crazy pissed off?"

"I don't know. I can't explain it; I just feel relieved. Angry and upset, yes, but most of all relieved." I sighed and thought about Lucia. And although I felt glad that he would be gone soon, I *was* pissed off that he had strung me along for all those years and betrayed me with another woman. In the immediate sense, I wanted him to suffer, but the deeper truth was that I didn't want to waste any more energy on him. He didn't deserve it. Lucia was my number one priority.

"How am I going to tell Lucia? Oh, and I told him I was packing his shit tomorrow and leaving it outside," I said, laughing nervously at my own boldness. Maybe I was losing it.

"Hey, I'll be here while you tell her, and I'll stay the night so I can help you tomorrow. Okay?" Susan grabbed my hand and squeezed. I nodded in thanks and looked around the room, making a mental list of what was his – what would be out the door come tomorrow.

Chapter 6
Hopscotch

It was Saturday night and time for my faithful call to my cousin and childhood friend, Lori. We kept each other informed on the latest gossip.

For instance, I knew Vitto was looking to move out of Boston and was shopping around for jobs. He had graduated from MIT and had a good job, but now he wanted a change. He was some sort of computer genius and made a ton of money.

Lori, two years younger than me, had gone to design school in New York when I started my junior year of college, and she had been living there ever since. She had met a wonderful man and married him a few years ago. Now she was working on her own label of clothes and trying to get it noticed. Most of the time when we spoke it was about fashion week and samples that she wanted to send me. She would say, "Mia, I found this wonderful fabric that would look great as a dress for you. I'm going to put it together and send it. I want you to model it for me and send me some pictures for my portfolio." And I did, every time. I had a lot of her original pieces, and her clothes were gorgeous.

Lori and I were the closest out of all of my cousins. Vitto came in second, even though he was a year older. I didn't talk to their brothers and sisters as often since they had been so much younger than us growing up. I moved away before I had the chance to bond with them. Our big Italian-American family was always in everyone's business. We didn't have to speak to everyone to let them know what was going on in our lives. All I had to do was tell my mother something, and the whole family would know the story in minutes. Likewise, I could call my mom on any given day, and she would know what they were up to, as well. She could dish out all of their stories to me, like how Vitto and Lori's younger sister, Monica, was already on her third kid at just twenty years old, or Lori's youngest brother kept getting suspended from school for fighting, or the second youngest brother had dropped out.

I sat on the balcony, curled on the lounge chair with a cup of tea and dialed Lori's number.

"It's about time you called," she said in her usual impatient manner.

I laughed and replied, "I just got Lucia down for bed. How are you?" I sipped my tea and scanned the olive trees surrounding my balcony.

"I'm good, but what I want to know is how *you* are."

I laughed at her Bostonian accent, wishing I still had mine. The minute I moved to Los Angeles, I worked to lose it so I wouldn't sound different from the other kids in school.

"I'm good, thanks. I've adjusted mentally and accepted that I am now in possession of a failed marriage," I said.

"Hey, stop that. You did nothing wrong."

"I considered that at first, but now I am wondering if I could have done something to change how the events played out. What's done is done, though. I know this."

I wrapped my hands around my teacup and cradled the phone between my shoulder and ear. A beautiful pair of gray doves landed on the teal green wooden banister at the opposite end of the balcony, and they sat looking back at me. Thinking about putting a bird feeder or birdhouse out for them, I recalled someone telling me that doves mated for life. What an interesting concept nowadays, I thought.

Placing the throw over my legs, I curled up on the chair a bit more tightly to battle the coolness of the night. "We've settled on everything," I continued. "He gave me half of everything except the house — that he left to me entirely. His attorney was pissed, but I guess Alex was trying to do something right."

"Ugh, that's just so wrong." Lori sounded disgusted. "So he's going to fill your pocketbook and pretend that takes care of all he's done?" she spat through the phone.

"I guess, but it's not like I had him around over the years anyway. I did everything on my own." I leaned my head back, trying to figure out what I had done to keep our marriage alive since Lucia had been born. I shook my head at myself in chastisement. And then I told her what I didn't want to believe myself: "God — and this is going to sound bitchy — but I didn't need him for anything, and, in all honesty, I've come to the conclusion that it was how I wanted it." I sighed at the truth. "I'll be set for a while. But he didn't want visitation rights at all. He said he didn't know Lucia before and doesn't want to now. That it's too late. Ugh! That's what has me so upset. Her own father doesn't want her. I mean who does that?" I gritted through clenched teeth.

All the stress I suffered during the divorce was centered around my daughter. The new, big lines between my eyebrows were from worrying about how Lucia would be affected.

"Excuse me?" Lori yelled.

I pulled the phone from my ear and smirked; leave it to my loyal cousin to be as upset as me.

"You heard me. I don't even think he'll ever want to see her. I think he's going to relinquish his rights altogether." I sighed and prepared myself for her reaction. "And don't yell, but I didn't ask for child support either," I whispered. If he didn't want her, I rationalized, then he shouldn't have to pay for her. She was mine, and I would care for her just as I always had: on my own.

ᕉᕉᕉᕉᕉ

Lori and her husband, Chris, were visiting for a week. We had plans to barbecue at the regional park on July third, which was when our neighboring city put on the fireworks show.

We spent the day before making all of the typical picnic food. My dad was responsible for reserving us a spot at the crack of dawn and for barbequing. Dad and I didn't spend a whole lot of time together, even though he lived in the same community I did. We both worked a lot, and when too much time passed without speaking, I'd call him and invite him over for dinner. He was a loner, and I was starting to believe I was turning out to be just like him in that regard.

When I'd first moved to California to live with him, we had gotten along just fine by staying out of each other's way for the most part. The physical affection we shared from my infancy was long gone after he left. Once we were geographically close again, he tried for a long time to hug and kiss me, but stopped after I rebuffed him too many times. Regardless of how much I chastised myself for doing it, knowing it hurt him, I couldn't stop. I just couldn't make the effort to show him much affection at all. Sure, we laughed and joked a lot and even did some fun things together, but our everyday activities were often done alone. He would go to work, and I would go to school.

Susan and my work friend, Danielle, her husband, and their seven-year-old son were going to spend the day with us, too. I had met Danielle at work and had fallen into an easy friendship with her. Recently, Lucia and I had spent a lot of time with Danielle and her family doing different activities. I thought from the moment I first saw her that Danielle was very beautiful. She was at least six feet tall with long legs and torso. Her tiny waist emphasized her small, high ass. She had the type of body that made women seethe in jealousy, and her striking, yellowish-green eyes were so different from anything I had ever seen. They were accentuated by her short, curly, blonde hair. Her sweet demeanor only added to her beauty.

Danielle was the one who had trained me and shown me around the airport. As a part-time administrative assistant for the customer service department, she had been with the company for a long time and knew the ropes. She was quiet in general, but in a one-on-one situation she would tell you her whole life story with little hesitation. Danielle liked to talk, but she was also a great listener. After she trained me and I got my bearings, I managed to show how much I was needed there. In a short amount of time, I was promoted to the position of administrative assistant to the general manager, after which they promoted Danielle to full-time administrative assistant as well. If we had time, we would meet for lunch and would help each other out when one of us was busier than the other. With her selfless heart, she never worried whether I was out to take her job. Her main concern was always making me feel welcome.

Gary, her husband of fifteen years, worked on the ramp as ground crew. Danielle and Gary had gotten married against their families' wishes when they were eighteen. They had made it a point to get their educations before they started to have children. From what I had seen with my own eyes and heard from Danielle, they were the envied happy couple. Gary was a nice, quiet man, though his large physique was a bit intimidating. He was at least six foot five, over two hundred pounds of sheer muscle. Big boned, he looked like a football player. He wore a crew cut that was already graying and had a mustache and goatee also sprinkled with white hairs. Gabe, their son, looked just like Gary. He was very tall for his age, almost as big as me, his head already reaching my shoulders.

It felt great to make more friends, and I couldn't wait to introduce this great couple to my cousin and her husband.

Chapter 7
Red Rover, Red Rover

I felt a warm body climb into my bed to snuggle, and I turned around to look at the clock. It was six o'clock in the morning and time to get up. Lucia curled into a little ball against my chest and went back to sleep, so I stroked her hair while I relaxed with her for a few moments.

When I was sure she had fallen back asleep, I got up and made my way to the bathroom. In a rush, I washed up so I could make myself a cup of coffee.

I popped a pod of butter toffee-flavored coffee into my Keurig, heated some milk in the microwave, and pushed the button to start the flow for eight ounces of water. That coffee maker had become a favorite of mine, because it could make a cup of fresh java within a minute. There were no more pots of coffee wasting away just to be thrown out after they burned from sitting all day.

The coffee was ready at the same time as the milk, and I put in a packet of Splenda. The first sip was always the best. Taking my cup, I padded my way to the balcony to relax outside for a few minutes of me-time before everyone woke up.

I was flipping through a magazine when someone opened the sliding glass door. When I turned my head over my left shoulder, I saw Lori carrying her own cup of coffee outside. She stepped over to the lounge chair next to mine.

I smiled at her and said, "Good morning." I was so happy to have her here.

Lori sat back and lay her head on the back of the chair. With a tired sigh, she said, "Morning,"

I laughed. "What's the matter? You didn't sleep well last night?"

She shook her head. "No, no, I did. I'm just not a morning person and still a bit jet-lagged. Oh, and Chris left around five this morning. Your dad picked him up so they could get us a good spot at the park," she said, and I nodded.

"Cool. My dad knows the whole routine and where we like to camp out for the day."

I considered their fatigue and the long day we had ahead of us. Fireworks wouldn't start until eight that night, and we'd be cooking, eating, and drinking all day.

"I hope Chris can last the whole day. We'll be there 'til about nine tonight," I told her.

She waved me off like she was swatting a fly and said, "He'll be fine. If he gets tired, he can just nap in a chair."

"Last year we put up a netted tent beside the Easy-up canopy, and I took a nap in there. That's an option instead of an uncomfortable chair." I chuckled.

I was a worrier, and I noticed that when things were quiet, my mind would start working a mile a minute. The lack of knowing what my future held made me crazy. I tried to lose myself in the calming coo of doves and the chirping of the small sparrows.

I thought about what was in store for Lucia and me. She would be starting first grade in September, and she had mentioned wanting to take ballet lessons. I wasn't sure how I would swing that time-wise.

I took one of my deep, sighing breaths, something I did when I needed to clear my thoughts.

"What's wrong?" Lori asked, pulling me from my internal musings.

Closing my eyes, I tried to put my thoughts into words. "I don't know," I shrugged, turned to look at her, and said, "I guess I was just trying to figure out how I was going to swing this coming school year with Lucia." I put my mug down on the small round table between our lounge chairs and turned to my side. "It's just that I'm not sure I can handle everything on my own. With Lucia getting older, she'll be busier. I'm beginning to feel overwhelmed, and I'm doubting my ability to continue to do this without help." I sighed again.

Lori sat up in a flash. The coffee swooshed in her mug, spilling a few drops on her sleep pants. It was so quick and unexpected that she startled me, and I jumped.

I put my hand on my chest and chuckled, out of breath. "What the hell, Lori? Are you trying to give me a heart attack? What is it?"

She put her mug down next to mine and was vibrating with excitement.

"Spill it!" I said, now curious.

"Oh, Mia, it's so funny how things work out. I have the perfect idea." She leaned forward to get closer, and instinctively, I leaned in toward her as well.

"Okay, so hear me out." She smiled to herself. "Chris's brother just lost his job on Wall Street. It's a long story that I'm sure he'll tell you himself, but he wanted a change. Something less stressful and more fun."

A doubtful laugh slipped from my lips, and I asked, "Um, when would he tell me, Lori? I don't know him."

"You will. So, anyway, he decided he wanted to be — a manny." She must have seen the confused expression on my face. "You know, a male nanny." Her eyes widened, willing me to catch on. She then waved a hand as if dismissing the whole thing. Whether I understood or not, she was going to continue with her story. "He asked a local agency in New York what the requirements were and began taking CPR, first aid, and some childcare classes."

I still had no idea why she was telling me all of this, but I sat and listened.

Lori jumped up to run inside. Before she got to the door, she began speaking under her breath in a muffled tone, "I need to call him before he signs a contract with that agency." Then she was gone.

What in the hell was that? I laughed because she just left me sitting there with no idea what she was talking about. Grabbing the mugs, I went inside. Lori was nowhere to be seen.

It wasn't until I was washing dishes that she came over and took a seat at the bar across from me.

"So, listen. This is a wonderful idea."

I dried my hands and stood opposite her, resting my forearms on the counter. "What in the world are you talking about? I have no idea what is going on," I said, a little frustrated.

"Well it's easy, Mia. You need a nanny — or in this case, a manny — to help you around here," she said with such conviction that I stopped mid-protest and began to think.

Did I need help? I hadn't even thought of hiring a nanny. The thought of having someone around to take her to ballet, tennis, and help with dinner would be nice. But I always had prided myself on doing everything on my own. To me, that was an accomplishment, and the thought of asking for help made me feel like a failure.

"Dominic needs a change, and moving here would be a perfect idea. I just spoke with him, and he is open to the offer." She clapped her hands together, and it was clear that she felt like her plan was coming together. "He is such a nice man who has had some unfortunate circumstances. He changed everything in his life because he was tired of the deceit and disappointment he dealt with on Wall Street," she said with sadness.

"What happened to him?"

"All I know is he was some kind of corporate finance specialist, the market crashed, his clients lost everything, and he was fired along with hundreds of others who worked with him." She shrugged.

"At first, he took it really hard. His fiancée left him. The money-hungry, gold digging bitch was just with him for his money and prestige. The minute he lost his job, she packed up and walked out." Lori shook her head, disgust written all over her face.

"Well, how would this work? I would want to meet him before I just hire him. I mean, I trust you and everything, but this is my daughter we're talking about!"

Lori sat up straighter and cut me off, mid-thought. "He can fly out here and meet with you, and if you like him, then he can meet Lucia. Dominic is ready to go anyway. He's already sold his house and has been staying with Chris and me." She smiled and continued. "He was going to put in an application with an agency called 'Mary Poppins.' After researching a bunch of agencies, he thought that one was the best."

Her smile was mischievous, the same one I remembered from our childhood. The more we talked and I watched her, the more I could see she hadn't changed much.

"So, you trust him? I mean, I know you said he's your brother-in-law, but this is my child."

Her eyes were soft, caring. "I would never put you in danger in any way. I love you both so much," she said, touching my hand.

I lowered my head to think it over for a moment. The fact was, I did trust Lori and her opinion. "Go ahead. Set it up." I smiled — with no idea what I was getting myself into.

Lucia woke up, and after a good breakfast, we decided it was time to bring the rest of the food to the park and join the guys.

Chapter 8
Miss Mary Mack

Lucia was excited for the day because some of her friends from school would be there.

"Lucia, help Momma carry this bag, please."

She grabbed it with both hands, hoisted it up in front of her, and carried it all the way to the car from the elevator. I couldn't help but laugh because I knew it was heavy, but my determined little girl still did it.

Lori, Lucia, and I found a parking spot far from our camp. The park was huge and was packed with many people, everyone dressed in summer clothes with some form of red, white, and blue on them. Some kids ran around with face paintings of fireworks and stars on their chubby cheeks. I was sure Lucia would want to join them.

We walked up and down the small hills on the way to our camp. The air was filled with the summery, delicious smell of barbeques; scents of hot dogs, hamburgers, and sunscreen filled my nose.

After a few minutes, we made it to our post and found the guys were already drinking beer.

I laughed. "Have you guys eaten anything yet?" I asked, giving my dad's shoulder a backhanded slap.

He grimaced at my playfulness and said, "Yes, missy, we did."

I nodded in approval. We didn't need them getting drunk before noon.

I looked around at the progress the guys had made. They had set up the Easy-up tent and the screened tent and had placed fold-up chairs, like those you would bring to kids' baseball games, all around in a circle. The barbeque was ready to go, and they had plenty of coolers to keep the food cold until it was time to start cooking.

"You guys did good," I said with pride. "Thanks."

I set all the salads and cold food into the coolers and surrounded them with ice. A long day in the sun would be bad for the mayonnaise, and I didn't want anyone to get sick.

It was pushing eleven o'clock, and so I asked, "When do you guys want to start cooking?"

My dad answered, "In a few. Don't worry; we've got it, honey."

Danielle, her husband, and her son arrived at eleven-thirty, and Susan came right after them. My dad had invited a few of his buddies, so they stopped by for a while.

Other friends of ours that had their own camps going stopped by for a quick chat. The day was nice and relaxing.

A short distance down the hill, on the lone flat surface big enough to hold it, was a big blow-up slide. Lucia was dying to test it out, and Danielle offered to take her along with her son, Gabe.

The sun was shining, and it was quite hot. We enjoyed our afternoon in the shade of the tents eating, drinking, and chatting sociably.

Once the sun set, the air was brisk, and we all put our sweatshirts on. It was getting close to the time the fireworks would start. We had to break down our camp area and store it back in the cars. As soon as the fireworks were over, the park would get crazy and everyone would be scrambling to leave.

With everything gone except our chairs, we sat and waited for the light show to begin. The kids were tired but excited. Lori, my dad, and I were sitting close together.

"Dad," I began.

He looked over at me.

"I was talking to Lori, and she made a good suggestion. I think I'm going to hire a nanny to help me with Lucia and some things around the house." I waved it off with my hand like it was no big deal. However, I still felt unsure about how hiring a manny would play out.

I wanted to tell him about my plan and get his opinion on the matter. I knew he cared about our safety, even if he came off as overprotective. I just needed support, another person to tell me this was the right thing to do. It didn't matter because the whole thing was already set up, and I was nervous.

His forehead scrunched up, and his eyes squinted into little slits. "Where are you going to look for someone like that? And are you sure you want the trouble?" His eyes darted to Lori's, then back to mine in a flash. "I mean, sometimes those things can be more headache than help."

"I know, Dad. It's just that I'm going to need help getting her from school and taking her to her activities and fixing dinner while I take her to ballet. I am always rushing to and from work so I can be where she needs me to be, and she is just going to get busier when she gets older. She wants to participate in all these activities, and I can't deny her." I hoped he would understand. "Lori recommended someone for the job, dad."

I watched Lucia running around in the grass with a multi-colored, light-up fairy wand, happy and carefree. Her curly, russet hair was halfway down her back, and her eyes sparkled like the waters in the Caribbean.

"Uncle Paul, Chris's brother lost his job and wanted a change. Dominic is who she's considering for the position," Lori broke in convincingly. "He's a great guy — a stand-up guy. I would never have mentioned it if I didn't think he was the best thing for Mia and Lucia."

My dad's eyes moved to Chris, and he asked, "What do you think about this?"

Chris stiffened momentarily at being addressed and then relaxed again. He was a reserved guy most of the time. "Well, my brother was dealt a shit hand and, without a doubt, wants a complete change. He's an honest man, and we have a damn fine 'pedigree,' if you will." He shrugged. "In my honest opinion, I think this whole plan will be beneficial for all of them. I have a feeling that they all will be better off in the long run. They can help each other," he continued with sincerity.

I jumped in as soon as he stopped talking. "I trust their judgment, Dad, and I know they'd never put us in a bad situation." While I bobbed my head up and down, I realized I was trying to convince myself as much as my father.

The lights began shooting up in the air and lighting the sky in red, white, and blue; it was breathtaking. I wrapped Lucia in my arms while she sat on my lap. I loved fireworks: the feeling of being free and childlike. Listening to all the "oohs" and "ahhs" just added to the excitement.

After the grand finale, we all kissed and hugged goodbye, with promises to get together soon. Then, as fast as we could, we folded up the chairs and made our way to our vehicles. The four of us piled into my car, while my dad went home alone.

જ્જ્જ્જ્

Lori and Chris's vacation ended much too fast for my liking, and I was sad to see them go back to New York. It always meant so much to me when my relatives visited; they were my connection to back home. I had always wanted a big family, and it was important to me that Lucia knew our relations and that she felt loved

Before she left, Lori arranged for her brother-in-law, Dominic, to arrive the following week for his interview. He reserved a room at the Marriot in the Fox Hills area, which was around the corner from my condo. I was nervous to meet him, especially since I needed to decide whether or not I wanted him to be a live-in nanny. It might be more convenient in the end to have him there all the time, but I worried about how I would separate his working time from his off time. Too many questions arose in my mind; I needed to do some research.

The day of their departure, I walked Chris and Lori to the security entrance to wish them a safe trip before they went to their gate.

"I'm going to miss you guys so much." I looked at Lori sadly. "Would you consider moving here?"

Chris shook his head with a deep chuckle. "I don't know. It's not that we don't like it here; it's just that our jobs keep us there."

I looked at Chris then, his body was tall and lean, and his skin was a dark olive color. He had short, black hair and colorful, hazel eyes. He was an okay-looking man, and it made me wonder what his brother looked like.

"I know, I just hate being here alone. Will you come and visit more often, then?" I asked with hope in my tone.

"We will — you know it. And I hope we can soon," Lori reassured me.

"I'll miss you." I hugged Lori with all my might, and then gave Chris a light squeeze. "Take care of her," I teased.

"I will."

Chapter 9
Duck, Duck, Goose

The next week flew by, and my nerves sent me into a whirlwind of cleaning. I spent the whole weekend scrubbing every inch of my condo and rearranging the guest room to look more masculine. Dominic wasn't staying here on this initial visit, but I wanted him to look at the room and feel like it could be a space he would want to stay in.

He was to arrive in town that morning at eleven, and it was now eleven thirty. Knowing he should be there soon, I walked around with a dust rag wiping down every surface, but I was still startled when the phone rang. Looking at the caller I.D., I saw that the call came from the guard-shack.

"Hello."

"Hi, this is Kevin from security. I have a Dominic Roberts here to see you."

"Send him in. Thanks, Kevin."

Lucia was at the park with my dad, who would bring her back in a while. I wanted to meet with Dominic before Lucia did, so the experience didn't scare her or confuse her. She still wasn't sure what a nanny — manny —was.

About fifteen minutes later, there was a knock on my door. When I opened it, I gasped, blinking. My mouth opened and closed several times, and I couldn't form a word.

The first thing I saw were his eyes, which were a shade that transcended the most beautiful green things in the world: peacock feathers, limes, and lush leaves. They were small, slanted, and topped with thick dark eyebrows, which added a hint of mystery. His hair was dark black and slicked back. The bone structure of his face was strong, masculine, and angled. I couldn't stop looking at him.

He cleared his throat and put out his hand. "I'm Dominic." I grabbed it in a firm shake, and I felt like I could see my future in that instant. Pictures of Dominic and me together in our old age flashed before my eyes. I felt comforted, as if I were wrapped in a warm coat of love. It was an amazing feeling.

After much too long of a handshake, I pulled my hand back and said, "I am so sorry, Dominic. Please excuse my manners." I waved him in with my right hand, while holding the door open with my left. "Come in. I'm Mia, by the way. Let's have a seat in the living room to talk."

I led the way to the sofa, and we both sat. I felt the need to explain myself, and the verbal vomit began. I turned bright red and said, "Please excuse my behavior at the door, it's just . . ." I looked up at him through my lashes, not trying to be cute, just truthfully embarrassed that I was going to be so honest. "It's just that you're beautiful."

I stood up in a flash when he paled before my eyes. His olive skin lightened to a pasty color. "Oh, God, I'm sorry. You want to leave, don't you? I don't act like this, usually. I swear I'm not crazy," I rambled. I turned away from him in embarrassment. God, this was one time when my big mouth was not productive.

Dominic stood up, walked toward me, and grabbed my shoulders, turning me to face him before saying, "No, I'm not leaving. I was just taken off guard, embarrassed." He grabbed my hand and guided me back to the sofa.

The whole situation had turned ridiculous. Leave it to me and my awkward behavior to ruin an interview with this . . . this . . . Adonis. I squeezed my eyes shut and filled my lungs with air. I tried a couple of cleansing breaths to start over, but it wasn't enough. "Excuse me, I'll be right back."

I walked like a bat out of hell to the bathroom, grabbed a washcloth from the drawer, and drenched it in cold water. Once I placed it on the back of my neck, it cooled me off in an instant.

Now, I needed to compose myself and not act like a teenager with raging hormones. With a big sigh, I smoothed down my blue tank top and pulled the hem over the waistband of my jean shorts. I made my way back out to the living room, still quite nervous, but ready to see if he was a good fit for Lucia's and my life.

With a very apologetic and sheepish smile, I said, "Dominic, I am so sorry. My behavior is very unprofessional. I hope we can start over." I could tell he was still sort of embarrassed, but he seemed much more comfortable after I spoke.

"It's quite all right," he said with a tilt of his head, making me feel better.

I knew that I would be calling Lori as soon as the interview was over. She would be getting a tongue-lashing for not warning me about how handsome he was. Once I got situated on the sofa again, I prompted, "So, tell me about yourself, Dominic."

He rubbed his palms on the front of his jeans and answered. "Well, I know Chris and Lori told you my story or at least the basics. So, after I lost everything, I needed to do something I knew I'd enjoy and that was very different than what I had been doing. I wanted to make sure it was something I could do as a career." He cleared his throat, which made me realize I hadn't even offered him anything.

I jumped up. "Can I get you something to drink? Water? Soda?" I asked.

"Oh, yes please. Water is fine." I jogged to the kitchen and pulled two water bottles from the refrigerator. Speeding back, I handed him one. He opened the bottle and took a long pull. His head was back and his throat exposed. I watched while his Adam's apple moved up and down with each swallow. *Shit, it's getting hot in here again.* Then I admonished myself. *Knock it off and pull yourself together.*

His beauty knew no bounds. He was perfection personified. My eyes scanned him from head to toe. His legs were long, clad in jeans, with a pair of black leather dress shoes peeking out at the bottom. He looked very clean cut in a blue short-sleeved, button-down shirt. With an attempt to cool myself off again, I took a couple of swigs from my bottle.

Dominic finished his water and put the empty bottle on the coffee table. "So,

34

after I decided I didn't want that lifestyle anymore, I thought long and hard about what I wanted to do. Before, I thought finances and stock markets were my life, but I learned that what I wanted more than anything was stability and a family." He breathed in a deep breath and closed his eyes for a long moment, calming himself.

"Anyway, after my fiancée walked out on me, I doubted I would ever have the chance to have the family I've always wanted. So, it seemed like the next best thing was to take care of someone else's. After I figured it all out, I begged my friends to let me watch their kids for them. It's not always easy, but it's been rewarding so far." His eyes bore into mine, pleading for me to understand and not to judge.

The one thing going through my mind was the desire to pull him into a hug and nuzzle him to my breast like a mother would. I wanted to soothe him, comfort him, and offer all that I had. Lucia and I could give him what he wanted. *Whoa, lady. Back up. You just met the guy.* I nodded in understanding, and the words just fell out of my mouth once again without my brain's consent. "Well, you can be a part of our little clan." I could feel my ears and cheeks heat up when I flushed. "I mean, that is, if you want the job." Could I blush any more?

Then I laughed when I realized I was getting ahead of myself. "Um, I suppose you should meet Lucia first." I looked at my watch and knew my dad would be there any minute.

Dominic laughed with me, showing he was just as nervous as I was. "Can you tell me about a normal day for you and Lucia, Mia?"

"Oh, sure. Monday through Friday, I work while she's in school, and then she goes to afterschool care until I get out of work." I took another sip from my water and continued. "I want to be involved as much as possible. I mean, I don't want to give over all of her care-taking to someone else.

I considered the live-in situation for a moment. "Would you consider being a full-time caregiver in our home?"

He nodded and answered, "I think that's best. That way I can be here for whatever she needs. Or you." His right hand gestured toward me. I looked into his eyes and smiled wide at the thoughts that flooded my mind. *Yeah, I might need something in the middle of the night.*

At that moment, I heard a key wiggle the doorknob and knew that my dad was home with Lucia. I stood suddenly as the excitement poured from me in waves. "She's here." I turned toward the door and waited for it to open, feeling more nervous than ever. Because I didn't want to see him go, I wanted nothing more than for Lucia to like Dominic. The thoughts I was having were unbelievable, but they were taking over. I felt a weird connection with him and I wanted to see where it could go.

The door flew open with a bang, and in bounced my little girl. Her pink, flowery shirt was stained with what looked like chocolate. My dad must have taken her for ice cream.

"Hi Lucia, Dad. I would like you to meet someone." I gestured to Dominic, who was now beside me. I looked at him, and his eyes were on my baby, sparkling with excitement.

Lucia, reserved for the moment, stood next to my dad waiting for something to happen.

"This is Dominic Roberts. Dominic this is my dad, Paul Balducci, and Lucia, my daughter." My dad and Dominic shook hands, and Dominic bent down to say hello to Lucia. "Hey, there. It's so nice to meet you. Your Aunt Lori told me all about you." His smile spread across his face.

She looked him in the eyes, shaking her head with a little pout and said, "She didn't tell me about you."

We all laughed.

"Hey, what's that?" He pointed at the chocolate on her shirt. When she looked down, he bopped her on the nose with his crooked forefinger. She cracked up as if that were the funniest thing ever. It was a great icebreaker. They hit it off from there.

I was still worried about what my dad thought, however. When Dominic stood up, I decided I would let my dad have his own chat with my new manny. "Lucia, come on. Let's get you washed up and change your clothes." I put out my hand, and she grabbed it.

Overall, the meeting went well, and I had a very good feeling about having Dominic there to help out with Lucia.

Chapter 10
Telephone

The next morning, as I sat on my balcony before Lucia woke up, I was able to relax and reflect. Mornings were my favorite time because I was able to relax and gather my thoughts before the day began. The quiet allowed me to breathe and to take in my surroundings. I sat there and reflected on my meeting with Dominic and my call to Lori the day after.

The day we met Dominic had gone so much better than I had expected. Dad gave me his approval of Dominic, and, to celebrate, I cooked us dinner, where I offered him the job. Dominic was excited and expressed his desire to work with us.

Now, the morning after he'd left, I had to make that call to Lori. I sat outside in my spot on the balcony with my coffee and the phone.

"Yes?" she answered.

"Is that any way to answer the phone, Lori?" I laughed.

"Well, I *do* have caller I.D., so I knew it was you."

"Fine. So, I have a bone to pick with you. Why didn't you tell me Dominic was so fine? Oh, my God, Lori. I think I've fallen in love." I chuckled.

She gasped. "Mia, are you kidding?"

And I laughed some more. "No, I'm not, Lori. Okay, yes I am, I think. I mean, how cruel to just let him show up and catch me off guard like that. You should have seen how foolish I acted."

She was laughing so hard that she couldn't even speak while she gasped for breath. "Well, I never paid attention to his looks. I mean I only have eyes for Chris. But I should have known he would catch your eye. What did you do when he arrived?"

I laughed and replied, "Well, I eye-fucked him when I opened the door, and it took about five minutes too long for me to snap out of it. That's so not like me. Once I realized what I'd done, I was so embarrassed, just acting like a love-struck teenager. He must think I'm a fool." *Although, he did accept the job,* I mused.

"In all seriousness, Lori I think I'm in love. When our hands touched, I saw flashes of a future of us together." I put my head in my hand at my ridiculousness. "I know, I sound crazy, but he seems like the perfect man for me, for us. And now I'm doubting my decision to have him here."

"Well, it sounds a bit crazy, but I understand. I mean when I met Chris, it was love at first sight. But, if you're feeling that way now, just pay attention and see how it goes. If he was afraid of your reaction to him, he wouldn't have taken the job."

I sighed and fidgeted with the tie of my bathrobe. "I guess you're right. I'm just worried I'm going to want more than he will. I don't think I could take the rejection after what Alex did to me. Dominic seems mature, and he wants a family, so I guess that's a plus. Well, I suppose I'll just wait and see," I muttered the last part.

"You'd be surprised, Mia. It all may just work out for you. Just see how he interacts with Lucia and go from there."

"Lori, he was wonderful with her. Here at the house, he engaged her in conversation and games. And at dinner, he helped me with her. He was very conscious of our norm and rules. Dominic would look at me for approval on things to make sure they were okay with me. It seems as if he will fit in just fine with her. She loved having a male figure around. I just worry that if it doesn't work she will get hurt," I said. I thought back to the previous evening.

After my dad and Dominic had a few words, I invited them to stay for dinner. I didn't want to send Dominic back to his hotel to spend the rest of the evening alone. I also wanted to watch him interact with Lucia more. Dominic agreed, but my dad had to leave. While I stood in the kitchen, preparing spaghetti with marinara sauce and garlic bread, I watched while Lucia bombarded him with random questions and information.

"Dominic, did you know I'm going to learn ballet? Dominic, do you want to play a game with me? You know I go to school? My mom says I'm smart." She went on and on, but I thought it was funny how Dominic did not seem flustered at all. He looked interested in and intrigued by her every word.

While I defrosted and warmed up the homemade sauce I had in the freezer, I heard Lucia talking about a candy board game she had.

"Dominic, you can be the green furry monster because his fur matches your eyes."

I laughed at that, because even she had noticed his beautiful peepers.

Dinner was almost ready so I popped the garlic bread in the oven.

"Lucia, I don't know how you do it. Look at where your character is and where mine is. I keep getting sent backward," said Dominic in mock surprise.

My baby laughed at him. "I don't know, but I'm win-ning," she said in a singsong voice.

"Okay, you guys, dinner's almost ready. Lucia, you want to show Dominic how to set the table?" I yelled out from the kitchen.

"Yes, Momma. Come on, Dominic, let's go." She got up, pulled him into the dinning room, and showed him where the place mats were and where to get the silverware.

So far, they worked well together. Dominic pretended to put the fork on the plate instead of on the placemat. Lucia had fun with that and playfully scolded him. "Hey, silly. The fork doesn't go there. See where I'm putting mine? It goes on the side."

"Wow, you're good at this." He smiled at her.

Peeking through the oven door, I saw the bread had turned a golden brown. "It's ready. Get drink orders, Lucia," I called out.

"Dominic, what do you want to drink?" she asked.

"Umm, water? How about you?"

"I'm gonna have milk. Momma, what do you want?"

"Water, baby, please."

While I placed the bread in a basket and plated the spaghetti, she asked Dominic for help pouring her milk. The bottles of water were easy for her to pour into glasses, so she did those on her own.

We all worked well together to get the meal on the table and sat down. Our usual seating arrangements had me at the head and Lucia to my left corner, but today she placed Dominic in that position and herself on the other side of him, far away from me.

Before we dug in, Dominic asked, "Do you say grace before dinner?"

"We do most of the time. It's Lucia's job, but if you'd like to, we'd be fine with it. Right, Lucia?"

"Yup, you can say it. I don't mind."

He nodded in agreement and looked thoughtful for a moment.

"Okay, let's hold hands." I held Dominic's hand, and he held Lucia's. "Thank you, Lord, for your gifts that we are about to receive. Thank you for bringing me into the lives of Mia and Lucia. Amen."

"Amen," Lucia and I said in sync.

"That was nice; thank you," I said. "All right, dig in, and later we'll have some dessert," I said, winking at Lucia.

She squirmed in her seat with excitement. "I love dessert," she said.

We must have been very hungry because there was not a lot of conversation. But I did watch as Dominic helped Lucia wipe sauce off her face, twirl the spaghetti onto her fork, and encourage her to finish all of her food so she could have the after-dinner treat I had prepared.

"I'm done," announced Lucia.

I smiled when I spied her empty plate and said, "Wow, great job."

Once Dominic and I finished, we cleared the table, and Lucia placed spoons and clean napkins by our placements.

I took three of my homemade chocolate chip cookies and warmed them in the microwave, and then topped them with a small scoop of vanilla ice cream. I also brought different types of sprinkles, jimmies, and chocolate syrup to the table. By the time Lucia was done with all of the toppings, we couldn't even see her ice cream. Dominic and I just used the chocolate syrup.

When Dominic was getting ready to leave, Lucia ran over to him and squeezed him with her little arms wrapped around his waist. He bent down to pick her up to give her a proper hug. They whispered to each other, and she gave him a smooch on the cheek. I stood off to the side watching. Even though I felt like I was an intruder on their newfound friendship, it was a wonderful ending to a pleasant beginning.

Lori shook me out of my reverie: "You can't predict what is going to happen, nor should you lose out on a great opportunity because of what might be. Just go with it. He's a wicked good guy, and I'd trust him with my kids if I had any."

And she was right. If he were good to my baby girl then I'd have nothing to worry about. I breathed out a big sigh, ready to start a new chapter in our lives.

☙ ☙ ❧ ❧

Sunday, Dominic's move-in day, arrived. Lucia was just as nervous and excited to have him come live with us as I was.

In his new room, I placed a basket with toiletries and brand new color-coordinated towels to match the decor. His bathroom and bedroom were decorated in chocolate brown, burnt orange, and a beautiful shade of teal, which seemed masculine enough for him. I put fresh, sweet-smelling lilies and tulips in his room, and the scent wafted out into the hallway, making the whole house smell delicious

I was both anxious and nervous for him to arrive. The refrigerator was stocked with enough fruits, vegetables, and meats to make dinner for about a week. Lucia's favorite strawberry yogurt sat in there as well. I had Lucia put her backpack, shoes, and the few toys she had in the living room, away in her own bedroom. She had made him a "Welcome Home" sign to make him feel comfortable. I had a set of keys made for the house and a key-card for the security gate ready for him. Also, I set up a binder with phone numbers and all of the information he might need. Lucia and I made him chocolate chip-oatmeal cookies and placed them in a decorative fashion on a fancy platter.

Dominic was supposed to come straight from the airport, which was about fifteen minutes away. We had arranged for SuperShuttle to pick him up and drive him to the condo. The service was cheap, and it allowed Lucia and me time to get everything ready. The phone rang, and Lucia began jumping around screaming, "He's here! He's here, Momma!"

I laughed as I reached for the phone. "Yes baby, I think he is." I picked up the phone. "Hello."

"Hello, this is Shawn from security, and Dominic Roberts is here."

"Send him in, Shawn. Thank you."

I turned to Lucia. "He's here. Get ready." She ran to get her sign so she could hold it up when he walked in the door. On the inside, I felt like jumping up and down too, but that would look ridiculous, so instead, I just waited in front of the door.

At last, he knocked, and I swear both Lucia and I ran for it. I reached for the knob while placing my right hand on my heart in an attempt to calm it down from beating so fast.

Taking a cleansing breath, I opened the door, smiling so wide my cheeks hurt. "Hi, Dominic." I waved him in. When I closed the door, I turned around and shot my eyes to Lucia so Dominic would notice the sign she was holding. Her arms must have been hurting from lifting it up so long.

"Hi, girls. Wow, Lucia. Is that for me?" he asked, and his eyes widened in delight. His smile was so beautiful. His lips turned up a little more on one side than the other. Adorable.

"Yes, it is. I made it all by myself." Lucia was so proud.

He walked over to her and looked at the sign she had so painstakingly made for him. I had written the letters on a separate piece of paper so she could copy them and write the sign herself. Then, she'd drawn flowers all around the letters, with a sun and bird at the top of the paper. She had taped two eight-by-eleven inch sheets of paper together to make it bigger. It was colorful and very pretty.

"It is so beautiful, Lucia. I love it so much. I'll keep it in my room," Dominic said in the sweetest tone.

Her curls bounced around while she clapped in excitement. She loved attention — most of all, male attention. I knew she wanted to make him proud, and I could tell by the look on his face that he was.

"Lucia, why don't you take Dominic to his room so he can set his things in there? I'm sure he wants to wash up and relax while I make us some lunch," I said. Then I looked at Dominic and asked, "You're hungry, right?" I nodded over exaggeratedly to get him to agree.

"Yeah, sure. I'll just go and put my things away," he said, picking up his bags and following Lucia to his room.

※ ※ ※ ※

The three of us sat around the kitchen bar comfortably and ate our sandwiches.

"How was your flight?" I asked before I popped a chip in my mouth.

"Long, but good. Happy to be here, though," Dominic said with a chuckle that resembled his brother's.

"Momma, can I have some more milk, please?" Lucia asked. She must have been hungry; she'd eaten most of her sandwich and drunk all her milk.

"Sure, baby." I pulled the milk from the refrigerator and filled her glass again.

"Thanks." She took a huge sip of her milk and was left with a big milk mustache. Lucia knew it, too, because she smiled so wide it stretched across her face. She was in a silly mood.

"Dominic, what kinds of fun things are we going to do after I get out of school?" she asked him with her broad grin. Giggles were about to burst from my mouth, but I tried to hold them in.

When he heard his name, Dominic looked at Lucia and noticed her mustache. He sucked his lips into his mouth to hold in his laughter. Once he had himself under control, he answered her. "Well, I'm not sure yet. I think you have ballet and homework; we'll have to figure the rest out together. How does that sound?"

With her forefinger tapping on her bottom lip in deep thought, she let out a sigh. "I guess so, but we'll have to find fun things to do."

"Here, wipe your mouth, silly girl." I handed her a napkin with a laugh.

"But, *Mo-om,* I like my mustache. Look — he has a little one," she said, pointing. Lucia was right. Dominic had some slight stubble on his lip and down his jaw. It was kind of sexy.

"Don't point. And that's enough. Clean yourself up and finish your milk, please," I said, putting an end to her growing silliness.

Dominic wiped his mouth and placed his crumbled napkin on his plate. His stood to walk his dish around the bar to the sink, but I stopped him.

"No, I'll do that." I gently took the plate from his hand.

He tried to pull it back, but I wouldn't give in.

"But I need to learn my way around here," he said with determination, and it sounded quite sexy.

I laughed because he was so cute. "Don't worry. You'll find everything in no time. The place isn't that big, and you'll be here all day. But today, I want you to relax. I'm sure you were up early to catch your flight."

With the plate in my hand, I felt smug for getting my way. Who knew how it would go after he'd been here for a while and got comfortable? Resigned, he sat at the bar again. Out of the corner of my eye, I caught him watching me while I worked around the kitchen. I didn't look him in the eye, because I didn't want him to know I'd seen.

"Yeah, I guess. I hate flying, though. Remind me to not do that too often. Oh, and by the way, I had some boxes shipped here a few days ago. Just a few things I didn't want to leave behind. I hope that's okay." When he rubbed his chin with his knuckles, I noticed his hands were almost feminine. His nails were well manicured, and his hands looked callus-free.

I scoffed. "This is your place now, too, so I want you make yourself at home here. Put your stuff wherever you want." I stopped cleaning the kitchen and stood across from him, leaning against the bar. Reaching into the basket on the bar, I pulled out his keys. "I have keys and a gate card for you here, and soon, I'll take you to Lucia's school with me so we can put your name on the paperwork. I want you to feel comfortable here." Then I looked at Lucia, who was sitting next to Dominic and watching us. "We're happy to have you here."

Chapter 11
Pin the Tail on the Donkey

Lucia's sixth birthday was approaching like a shot, and I had nothing planned. After some thought, I decided that the easiest solution would be a small gathering at Chuck E Cheese. Lucia was excited when she found out where we were having her party. We invited some of her friends from school, plus Danielle, Gary, Gabe, Susan, my dad, and Dominic and me.

I found a wonderful bakery near our house that made the most amazing cakes and ordered one for Lucia that was decorated with pink ballet slippers and lots of pink frosting.

Lucia wanted to wear a dress that looked like a ballet costume. We searched high and low and found an adorable dress with a white bodice covered in pink polka dots and a big puffy skirt with lots of pink and white tulle. She wore little white shorts underneath the dress since she would be climbing in and out of the tunnels and I didn't want her showing her undies to everyone. Her hair was up in a tight ballerina bun, and she sported a pair of old ballet slippers.

Sometimes when Lucia needed to run around and let off steam, we would go to Chuck E. Cheese so I could sit and relax. I would bring a book and sit in a booth, and she could come and check in with me every few minutes. It was a great playground for allowing the kids freedom to play without the parents suffering from fear of kidnapping. The system was genius. At the entrance, an employee stood stamping the hands of families that entered together. The stamp had a number for each family and was invisible on the hand. When it was time to leave, the employee would place the parent and child's hands under a black light to see if the numbers matched. If they did, they could all leave together, but if the numbers didn't match, they could not leave. It made it a safe place for kids to play.

The staff had set up a long table in the party room. The room had a stage filled with some mechanical characters — friends of Chuck E. himself — holding band instruments, and every hour on the hour they would break out into song and dance. Every few minutes, a parent would come into the party room and drop off their child and ask what time they needed to come back for them. Almost all of her friends were there.

Susan and my dad arrived at the same time with their hands full of bags.

I took a good look at what they had in their arms. "What's with all the bags?" I pointed to them.

"They're Lucia's gifts." Susan smiled like the little devil she was.

"What? No way, Susan," I said shaking my head back and forth "That's too much. You can't give her all of that." My voice was adamant. She was going to spoil her.

"It's just one big gift that comes in a lot of small packages. Relax."

My dad made quick work of pulling the small wrapped gifts out of the bags and setting them on the table.

"Hi, Dad." I reached up and pecked his cheek.

"Hey, kiddo. Where's the birthday girl?" He looked around for Lucia. I laughed because he'd never find her in that crowd of little heads running around. The place was packed, and all of her friends had arrived. Even though the kids were running around playing in the game room, they'd stop what they were doing and run back to the party room to watch the performance on stage. It was always the same song, but the kids loved the show regardless.

I answered my dad: "She's around somewhere playing. I gave all the kids their coins, so I'm sure they're hitting up the machines for tickets."

He nodded and took a seat.

"Do you want a beer?"

His eyes lit up. "They serve alcohol in this place?" he asked with hope in his voice.

"Yeah, how do you think the parents survive all of these kids? They need a little bit of help." I laughed.

He gave me a deep laugh in return and said he'd take a beer ASAP. I looked around for Dominic and saw his head in the sea of games. He was surrounded by a ton of little children, who were screaming and jumping up and down with pure excitement while they played.

While I stood in line for my dad's beer, I felt someone barrel into my legs from behind and looked down to see Lucia.

"Momma, you should see all the tickets Dominic won me. So many! I can pick a good prize!" she screeched with excitement.

"Wow, baby. That's wonderful. Make sure you thank him for playing with you guys." I brushed back the wisps of hair that were falling out of her bun. She was wearing a small princess crown that I hadn't seen before. "Where'd you get the crown?"

Lucia touched the top of her head as if she'd forgotten it was there. "Oh, Dominic gave it to me. He said I was the princess today."

My heart just swelled. He was so sweet to us.

"That's because you are."

My eyes roamed the room until I found Dominic at a machine, surrounded by Lucia's friends. I wanted to go to him. Over the small amount of time he'd been living with us, I was drawn to him like we were magnets constantly pulling toward one another.

I paid for my three beers and delivered one to my dad. "Thanks, kiddo," he said taking a huge gulp after I placed his mug on the table. I'd found him sitting in the party room talking to Danielle, who had just arrived. I gave her a big hug. "Hey, girl. Thanks for coming."

"Excuse me, guys. I'll be right back. I need to deliver this." I held up one of the mugs while taking a sip from the other.

Walking toward the last place I'd seen Dominic, I found him a few machines over. I could feel my face light up when I looked at him. He was so sexy, and yet, there he was playing with a bunch of six-year-old girls and having a great time doing it. I began to rush over to him, and then, all of a sudden, shyness washed over me and I slowed my pace until I reached him.

I cleared my throat. "Hey, having fun?"

He looked over his shoulder and smiled wide.

I felt myself blush. "Thirsty?" I croaked.

Turning around to face me, he reached out for the beer. "Thanks. This is perfect."

My eyes were glued to him while he gulped down his beer. Going through the motions without thinking about it, I followed his example and guzzled mine as well.

"*Sooo*, are you going crazy yet?" I teased, trying to flirt a little without seeming obvious.

He let out an incredulous gasp. "No way! I'm having a blast. I don't think I've ever been to a Chuck E. Cheese before, and this is incredible for the kids. Plus, I'm trying to win Lucia a ton of tickets. She said she gets to pick a toy with them," he whispered the last part as if it were a secret. Lucia knew how to work it; she could coax anyone into winning tickets for her.

"Well, that's super nice of you." We placed our empty mugs on the empty table behind us and stood side-by-side playing games together. I was having a lot of fun myself.

Dominic dragged me, Lucia, and some of the kids who were playing near us to the Skeeball lanes, at which he turned out to be really good. My own Skeeballs were bouncing all over the place — half the time ending up in his lane. Full body laughs wracked us, and he'd hip check me every time my ball would interrupt his game.

"Wow, Mia. You're pretty bad at this. Here, let me show you." I gasped, pretending to be hurt, because he was laughing at me. When he lined his body up behind mine, placed his left hand on my hip and his right hand over mine, I forgot everything else. With the ball in my hand, he showed me how to swing and aim at the hole for the highest score. And what a team we made; the ball made it in every single time he helped me. When I tried on my own, I didn't do as well, which was quite all right with me since I loved the feel of him pressed against me.

Three hours later, after a song and dance from Chuck E. Cheese, pizza, the happy birthday song, tons of sugar-filled cake, and gifts, Lucia was wiped out. So were Dominic and I. Lucia was very appreciative of all her gifts, but her favorite was what Susan brought for her. She'd screamed and squealed while she opened every single one of the little packages to reveal a beautiful three-story dollhouse with all of the accessories: furniture, people, decorations, paint, and small sheets of wallpaper. It was a thoughtful gift that would keep her busy for a long time. At the end of the party, my dad looked like he was going to have a nervous breakdown from being around so many crazy kids. He was good at entertaining with adults, but he didn't have much patience for so many children. He loved Lucia to death, but he was only putting up with her antics for this long because she was his family.

The wonderful thing about having a party at an establishment like Chuck E. Cheese was there was no clean up for me. And once it was over, I was done.

Chapter 12
Double Dutch

September arrived before we knew it, and school started for Lucia. Dominic went with me the first day so he could learn the routine and the location. He had purchased himself a car to get around the first week he was here, a nice BMW 328i.

I imagined it wasn't what he was used to compared to his previous experience in high society. The more I thought about it, I didn't even think he drove too much in New York. He seemed well adjusted, not just to what he drove, but to his new life. In all the time he'd been here, I couldn't picture him in his old life at all. He fit with us.

I told Dominic to drive so he could get a feel for where everything was. When we arrived at the school, we all piled out, Lucia was excited to have Dominic with us, and she dragged him to her line. She pointed out all of her friends and the location of her classroom and the lunchroom. Dominic took it all in, and even asked her questions to encourage her even more. I loved how much he nurtured her outgoing personality.

Once the kids had gone into their classes, we went to the office to add Dominic to the list of authorized people for emergencies and pickup. Even though he was my employee, something about these changes and additions made me tingle with excitement. In my mind, it was as if he was inching his way into our lives more and more, one change at a time — and I was very happy with that.

On our drive back to the house, he asked, "Not to get personal but, where is Lucia's dad?"

I glanced over at him for a moment, trying to judge his expression. I wondered why he was asking. "Um . . . he's not around." I looked at Dominic once more to gauge his reaction.

He snuck an encouraging look at me, and then flashed his eyes back to the road.

"We were married, but he was never around. He worked all the time. Lucia didn't even know him. He told us he was working to give us a better life. It was a crock of shit." I snorted, shaking my head. "I mean, we had known each other as kids. And once we met up again and got married, I think we mistook our common past for love. Things changed when he started his job; from then on, it was always about work. The attentive, sweet man I knew was gone. I kept hoping he would settle down and put us first, but he never did. I realized he never would," I said. "He was having an affair. I kicked him out, and he just walked away without looking back." I shrugged.

Dominic nodded and met my eyes again.

"I suppose what stings most is that I have a failed marriage on my record. I mean, that's the one thing I wanted to do right. My parents divorced when I was young, and I wanted to find 'the one' and prove that I could stay married." I snorted at the absurdity. "The other thing — and this hurts more than anything in the world — is that he relinquished his parental rights with Lucia." I shook my head in disgust.

"I don't understand how he could just walk away." Dominic's lips were set in a grim line.

He was quiet, and I noticed the lines on his forehead were pulled tight like he was thinking. His clenched jaw made him look angry, but he didn't say anything more.

I figured this would be a good time to get the exes out of the way. "So, Lori told me a little about your fiancée. What happened with you two?"

His eyes flickered to mine. Taking a deep breath, he then released it with a quick puff.

Shrugging, he said, "She left when I lost my job. She was more interested in my connection to the social circles in New York and my money than in me. When I told her I was not going to look for another job in that field, she packed up and left without a word. She didn't even want to hear me out or try to understand why I wanted a new career. I was burned out, tired of the fast pace without the rewards. I mean, I gave my life to that company, and they kicked me to the curb the moment things got tough." He rubbed his knuckles across his chin a few times and continued. "The thing was, I had my career all worked out. We were going to get married, and I wanted to start a family. I wanted that, and I thought I was going to have it with her. I should have known she was shallow. I should have seen it, but I suppose being on the inside blinded me, and I couldn't see what was going on."

I snorted. "I know just what you mean. I should have demanded Alex lay off his job a lot sooner or left him if it didn't change, but I got caught up as well. I tried to be the supportive wife without the nagging, and look where it got me. But what makes you think you should have known she was shallow?"

I caught him frown out of the corner of my eye. "With Porsha, she always wanted to one-up her friends, had to have the nicest things, and be seen in the most exclusive places. To say that I was a financial advisor on Wall Street was a big thing, and she loved bragging about it. I guess I just ignored those self-centered behaviors of hers."

Dominic cleared his throat and rubbed the back of his neck with his right hand. "By the way, you didn't fail at your marriage, Mia. You failed in your choice of a husband. You still have a chance at a successful marriage; you just need the right man."

ৡৡৡৡৡ

The three of us formed a routine with ease and adjusted well. I arrived home after work one day, and the scent outside the door was delectable. The smell of onions, mushrooms, and garlic wafted out into the hallway. The muffled sounds of Dominic giving Lucia instructions and her responding giggles put a smile on my face.

The front door opened right next to the kitchen, so I opened it as quietly as I could to spy on them. Dominic was a wonderful cook, and he had been teaching Lucia. I thought it was a great idea for her to learn at her age, and she was so eager to participate in anything Dominic wanted to do with her.

The scene I walked in on made my heart beat faster. Lucia was kneeling on one of the bar stools, using her little fingers to spread crust in a pie pan. After her fingers would push down on the dough, her thumbs would smooth it out. The tip of her dark pink tongue peeked out of her closed, rosy-red lips. A lined formed between her eyebrows, showing her deep concentration. If she knew I was standing there watching her, she made no move to acknowledge me. Instead, she looked at Dominic with a serious expression, held the pie plate up, and said, "Like this, Dominic?"

He had his back to her, stirring something at the stove, and when he turned around to see what she was showing him, his eyebrows raised in surprise. "Wow, that's perfect. She's going to love it." He reached over and grabbed a bowl to set it in front of Lucia. "Okay, now use this spoon to put the pudding on top of the crust." Lucia pulled the bowl next to her pie plate and began scooping and smoothing until she had used the entire bowl of filling.

"Okay, I'm done. What's next?" she asked, so happy that she was learning and participating in daily tasks with someone besides me.

Looking around and spotting me standing by the front door, Dominic turned back to Lucia. "How about you say hello to your mother?" he said with a smile that lit his whole face.

Before I looked back to Lucia, I noticed Dominic was dressed in some tight True Religion jeans, a white T-shirt, and bare feet. He was sexy as sin, but I couldn't say anything about it yet. He had made no move toward me at all since he had arrived, and although a lot of what he did seemed like a form of courting, there was no real indication of interest, so I would just have to sit and wait. I was not going to make the first move because I was so afraid of screwing this up and chasing him away. Now that we had him, Lucia and I would not survive without him. I knew it deep in my soul.

"Momma!" yelled Lucia before she jumped down from the stool and ran right into my arms. Pulling her close, I sprinkled kisses wherever I could reach. I pulled her back so I could see her face and snuck one last kiss to her nose.

"What are you two doing?" I asked.

She squirmed to get down, and as soon as her feet touched the ground, she grabbed for my hand and pulled me into the kitchen. I spied Dominic putting the pie in the refrigerator. "Hi, something smells divine," I said, feeling shy all of a sudden.

He still had that beautiful smile on his face. "Oh, nothing. We just made dinner. Why don't you go put your stuff away and come back so we can eat?" He stood behind me and lifted my jacket from my shoulders. I slid out of it, and he hung it in the closet.

"Thank you; I'll be right back." I went to my room, changed out of my work clothes, and threw on a Guess sweat suit. I wanted to rush back out so as not to miss a moment with those two, so I sped through washing my face and brushing my teeth.

Lucia was sitting at the table with all the patience she could muster, while Dominic was in the kitchen pulling clean plates out of the oven. He had been thoughtful enough to heat up the plates to keep the food warm while we ate. As soon as she spotted me, Lucia called me to the table, and then yelled to Dominic, "She's here!"

"Can I help?" I asked.

"Oh, no! You sit down and let me do this for you," Dominic answered with an adorable smile. He had so many smiles, and every one of them was amazing. Every time I looked at him, my head would spin — he was so swoon-worthy.

I couldn't deny him, so I went to sit with Lucia. Stage-whispering to her, I asked, "Hey, what's the occasion?" She just looked at me like I was crazy. I didn't think she quite understood what I was asking. "I mean, what's going on?" I waved around to the table.

She perked up and answered, "Oh, its dinner. We cooked for you." For some reason, I still felt like they were up to something. I was having a hard time not laughing at her cuteness.

Dominic served us, setting down our plates in front of us, and then took a seat. Our meal included baked potatoes, sautéed vegetables, and steak cooked with mushrooms and onions. He poured Lucia some sparkling apple juice and held up a bottle of wine to ask me if I wanted any. I nodded in response.

In that moment, I was so grateful for having him in my life, knowing I would be overcome with that same feeling a million times more. Although I had always appreciated the small things in life, with him, I appreciated them so much more. The three of us sat there, Dominic at the head of the table, Lucia and I on either side of him, and we said grace. Holding his hand, I gave silent thanks for sending him to us.

Chapter 13
Musical Chairs

Dominic kept himself busy during the day reading or cleaning around the house. He did our laundry, which I was quite embarrassed about the first time I noticed. I didn't want him to think he was our maid, but he insisted that it was not a problem and promised me that he took time for himself. He wanted to do whatever he could to make my life easier, which I thought was sweet.

During the weekends, at Lucia's insistence, he would join us on our usual expeditions to the zoo, the park, or museums. I didn't want him to feel obligated, but secretly, I did want him with us. I enjoyed his calming company. He told me over and over again how he wanted to spend time with us, and I believed him. It was a nice change in our lives.

One Saturday morning in late September, Susan called me while I was making some coffee. Her enthusiasm was much too much at that time in the morning.

"Hello," she said in a singsong voice.

"Wow, you're up early. What're you doing?" I asked.

She made a noise of dismissal and said, "I've been up since the ass crack of dawn. I couldn't sleep. But I want to go with you guys to the zoo today. Are you still going?"

"Of course you can join us. Dominic is going, too. I hope that's okay."

"Woo hoo, I get to spend some time with the sexy manny. You hitting that shit yet?"

I inhaled quick and deep. "Susan, don't be so crude. And no! God, do you have any shame?" I huffed out, quite exasperated.

"Pft, ummm . . . no. I don't know what's taking you so long. I'd have hit that sexy piece of man meat a long time ago."

"That's not funny. It's not cool that you're talking about him that way. Knock it off."

She blew out a long whistle. "Oh, I think someone has the hots for her manny," she taunted, cracking herself up.

"So, you mentioned something about not sleeping. What's wrong?" I said to change the subject. I didn't like her talking about him like he was just a "piece of meat" to me.

"Oh, okay. Fine, I'll lay off this time. I was going over a heavy case I'm working on. It's pretty insane, and it's kept me really busy, which is why I'm looking forward to a day of fun."

"Well, I hope the case works out for you. And I'm glad you're coming, but please don't tease Dominic. We're not like that," I pleaded.

I heard her sigh, and I knew she was pouting because I had ruined her fun. "So, I'll see you in an hour. I'll meet you there, okay?"

"Perfect. See you then."

An hour later, we arrived at the Los Angeles Zoo. Lucia was bouncing in her booster seat while Dominic helped me out of the car. When he opened my door for me, I couldn't help but stare up at him with wonder. Did he do these things for me just because he was a gentleman, or was there more meaning behind these gestures? Did he feel it was his job? God, I was so confused!

He stood there in his patient manner, waiting for me to get myself together. After I'd grabbed my purse, I held out my left hand for him to assist me out of the car.

"Thank you."

With a nod of his head, he helped me out. Then he closed my car door and opened Lucia's for me. I undid her buckles, and she hopped out as quick as a bunny. Not giving us a chance to do anything else, Lucia grabbed our hands and dragged us toward the entrance.

Susan was waiting at the ticket booth, and before I could introduce her to Dominic, she scooped up Lucia and hugged her.

"Auntie Susan, too tight!" Lucia gasped, sounding out of breath.

"Hi, my little girl. How're doing?" Susan asked while letting Lucia get down.

"Good, Auntie Susan," replied Lucia.

I began introductions, the whole time burning a hole in Susan's head with my eyes, hoping she would remember to behave.

"Dominic, this is my best friend—not that I know why most of the time— but she is, nonetheless. And, Susan, this is Dominic." Leaving the manny part out felt right; he wasn't one today, and I didn't want him to think that was all I thought of him.

I knew she wouldn't keep her promise. A wry smile spread across her face, and she caressed his arm while she shook his hand. "It is so nice to meet you." Flicking her eyes to me then back to him, she continued. "Mia has told me *so* much about you," she said with a sweet, sarcastic voice.

Dominic's eyes flashed to mine, and then a huge smile formed on his mouth. "It's nice to meet you, too," he said, making eye contact with me rather than her.

"Come on, everyone. Let's go!" screeched Lucia.

"Great idea, baby. Let's get in there. I want to see the elephants. How about you? What do you want to see?"

"I want to see the monkeys, Momma."

Flies and bees swarmed us while we stood by the fence watching the elephants. The sun was hot and mixed with smells of animals, making the experience feel a little overwhelming. It was all worth it, though. I knew that Lucia was enjoying her day. We were in great company, and none of us could get enough of watching our favorite animals. Susan watched Dominic and me like a hawk; I supposed she was trying to read something more into what was between us. She was ridiculous; every time he moved, her eyes were on him.

I watched Susan's eyes follow Dominic's every move when he offered to buy Lucia Velcro hugging monkeys, and me a plush elephant with a squeezable heart on its chest. She watched while he held Lucia's hand most of the day and when he placed his hand on my back to allow me to go before him in doorways. Her smirk grew when he passed me the ketchup at lunch and held onto my hand for a moment too long. I knew I was going to hear all about it later, but as long as she didn't embarrass us here, I didn't care. All the same, I could tell she was impressed with him and his attentions toward Lucia and me.

The whole outing was fun. Toward the end of our day, I noticed Susan took a moment to have a conversation with Dominic that, by the expressions on their faces, seemed serious. Knowing her meddling personality, I imagined she was giving him permission, as my best friend, to pursue me.

ডে ডে ৶ ৶

My baby girl had attended her first ballet class a few weeks ago, and she was obsessed with it now. She was serious about her instruction and practiced all the time.

"Lucia, come on, sweetheart; it's time to go." I lifted her pink ballet bag over my shoulder.

She turned the corner from her room into the hallway in her pink leotard, tights, and tutu. Dominic had learned to style Lucia's hair, and today he had pulled it into a tight bun.

The first time he asked me to teach him how to do her hair, I had finished showering after putting Lucia to bed and had gone to the kitchen to make some hot tea. Dominic heard me and sat across from me at the bar.

"Um . . . Mia?"

I looked up at him. His eyebrows were scrunched, and his cheeks pinked a tad.

"Yeah? What's wrong?" I asked. His fingers were fidgeting on the counter, and it was beginning to worry me. Was he going to quit?

"Well, I was wondering if you could show me how to do Lucia's hair. Because . . . umm . . . there are times when she goes to ballet and she wants it in a bun. I have no idea how to do that. So, do you think you could show me?"

My heart began to flutter; he was so sweet and considerate.

"Of course, do you have time now?" I asked. Watching him drum his fingers made me want to reach out and hold his hand.

"Well, yeah." He shrugged. "I mean, I have nothing else to do and if you're not busy right now . . ."

Forgetting the tea, I began walking to my room to get my brush and some hairbands. "Wait here. I'll be right back," I called from my doorway.

I came back out with what I needed and walked over to the couch. "Come on, sit on the sofa." Once he did, I sat on the floor between his legs. "Okay, so first. When you brush long hair, you have to remember that it gets tangled. You don't want to just run a brush through it and yank it out. It will hurt and make any girl scream at you," I said with a laugh.

Looking at him from over my shoulder, I gathered all of my hair at the nape of my neck and showed him how to brush it from the bottom and work his way up.

"So, once you're sure you have all of the tangles out, you can brush from the top. But be careful you don't make more knots in it. Now, it's your turn."

I watched while he nodded and took the brush, and then I turned around so he could start.

"Just brush my hair to get the feel for how you would start with Lucia," I said, trying to soothe his nerves.

His gentle hands worked light strokes over my scalp and down my mane. It felt so good and relaxing that I was almost falling asleep. I let him spend a lot of time with the brushing for selfish reasons, but before I could show him how to pull it up into a bun, I felt him gather my hair near my nape. His fingers skimmed my neck, either by accident or on purpose, sending shivers through my body. I wasn't sure if he meant to do that, but I didn't want to stop him. He continued to run his fingers through my hair, forgetting the brush altogether, and my eyes began to close.

Realizing I was falling asleep and I hadn't shown him anything more than how to brush my hair, I decided it was time to get into the difficult stuff.

"That felt good, but let's start with the hairstyles. Let me see the brush, please."

He handed it to me, and keeping my back to him, I showed him how to brush the hair up into a ponytail in the back and secure it with an elastic band. After a couple of tries, he got it all and secured it without leaving any bumps of hair around my head.

"What were you like as a kid?" Dominic asked out of nowhere.

"Oh, well, you know Lori and I grew up in Boston, right?"

"Yeah, I knew that," he confirmed.

I shrugged, not knowing exactly what he was looking for. "I don't know. I was a tomboy. I never let the boys tell me I couldn't do something just because I was a girl. How about you?"

"Let's see. I never got to play outside. We lived in Manhattan, so we had a concrete garden, but my parents were too serious for kid stuff anyway. They treated us like adults from a young age, and we didn't know any better. But I played sports, at least; Chris never wanted to. He was always more serious than I was, which seems almost impossible. I can see how uptight I was and how much I've loosened up since I've left New York," he explained.

"So, you never got to play hide and seek as a kid?" I thought about that and realized it wasn't that different for Lucia, either. Even though we had the grounds outside to play in, we never did.

"Nope, never."

"Well, neither has Lucia. We'll have to play by the lake sometime."

"You didn't go to Lori and Chris's wedding, did you?" Dominic asked.

I shook my head. "I couldn't. The timing wasn't right, but I was upset that I missed it."

"It was beautiful. My parents invited all of their friends, and your aunt and uncle were there with their other children. It was a good time, but so many people. I expected Lori to be overwhelmed, but she handled herself well."

I wished I could have been there for Lori. That was something I could never make up to her, and it bothered me all over again.

After that, we spent several more hours talking while he brushed my hair, practicing making ponytails, buns, and braids. The feeling of his fingers running through my hair and skimming against my neck sent tingles down my spine. This man enticed me with even the simplest action, but I felt like that evening we'd shared something more. I looked forward to many more moments like that with him.

"I'm ready," Lucia said while smoothing down her tutu.

Before every session, Lucia would rush us to the studio ahead of time so she could stretch and get a good spot at the barre.

Dominic held his hand out for her to hold when we headed out the door. He helped her into the car and opened my door before running to the driver's side. Once we were in the car and buckled in, Lucia began chatting away.

"Dominic, today we are going to learn a new routine. Mrs. Caprisi said it's for a 'cital. She said we hafta practice a lot to make a good show."

I chuckled at her excitement and loved to hear her talk; however, I was beginning to feel a little jealous at how much she addressed Dominic all the time instead of me. Although I knew it was foolish, just a small part of me felt it and it hurt—felt strange, because I'd never had to share her before. I caught Dominic's smile; he knew I was brooding.

I turned to look at Lucia. "Do you know what a *recital* is, Lucia?" Continuing to look at her over my shoulder, I saw her face scrunch up in thought.

"Um, I'm not sure."

I smiled because she was so excited over something just because it had to do with dancing, even though she didn't know what it was.

Dominic made a right turn onto the street of the studio. "Well, it's a show to demonstrate to your family and friends everything you have learned. We get to see you dance with your classmates in pretty costumes. It's a very exciting night," he answered.

He pulled into the parking lot, and Lucia seemed to be in deep thought.

"We hafta dance in front of people?" she said, and her voice trembled.

Once he parked the car, he jumped out and helped Lucia out. I stood behind him and said, "Baby, does that make you nervous?"

She nodded.

Dominic pulled her out of the seat and held her to his chest. He hugged her and stroked her hair. "It's okay to be nervous. Even the best dancers in the world get nervous before they perform. But if you practice hard and try your best, you will be just fine. No matter what happens, we will be proud of you."

She pulled back a little and looked up at him with watery blues and said, "I'm ascared that you and Momma won't like my dancing, and if I make a mistake, you'll be mad."

"Oh, sweetheart, we all make mistakes. We would never be mad at you for that. All you can do is try your best and have fun. We love you so much." He hugged her tight again and kissed her forehead before I ushered them inside the studio. Moments like those made my heart skip a beat, and I tried not to cry while we ran into the studio.

Inside, the walls were covered in mirrors, and across the middle were stretching barres. On one of the walls, the barres were shorter to accommodate the little children. Because it was the first time I had been able to attend a lesson, Dominic showed me the ropes. The parents sat by the entry of the studio in folding metal chairs. The scent of baby powder and sweat hit me; it was quite soothing.

If it weren't for Dominic being here with us, Lucia wouldn't have been able to participate in anything after school. Watching Lucia concentrate so hard on what she was doing and enjoying the activity just reinforced how right it had been to hire him.

Chapter 14
Four Square

I introduced Dominic to my friends, Danielle, Gary, and their son, Gabe. We invited them over for dinner, and Dominic immediately became close with Gary. Every once in a while on a Friday, they would go shoot pool and have some beers. I felt that it was good for Dominic to get out and make friends besides Lucia and me.

Dominic got along well with Susan, too, even though she teased him to death, and my stomach fluttered when she told me later that he seemed interested in me. I wasn't sure of his interest level, but we did fit together pretty well. If I were honest with myself, I would admit to that I did notice something that seemed to be more than friendship, but I did not want to get my hopes up. The tasks he performed around the house for us were part of his job, and although he went above and beyond the call of duty, I thought that was just his way. He was kind, generous, and helpful, even when he was not asked. The two of us seemed to live like a couple without the intimacy, and I figured I would let nature take its course. I didn't want to rush into anything or force it.

On a Friday night while Dominic was out with Gary, my cousin, Vitto, called me to let me know he would be flying out to Los Angeles for some interviews. It had been years since I'd seen him last, and I was dying to catch up. We planned to meet for dinner and drinks, and my dad agreed to babysit Lucia that night so I could take Dominic with me.

My cousin was in town, and I had been telling Dominic for days that I wanted him to go out with us.

"Are you sure you want me to go?" he asked, leaning against the hallway doorjamb. He had just showered and his thick black hair was wet and sticking up in all directions. Pictures of him wet and naked in front of the bathroom mirror, rubbing the towel back and forth over his hair to dry it flashed through my mind. His light purple button-down shirt made his green eyes stand out even more, and it looked good against his bronzed skin. I couldn't help checking him out from head to toe and, by the look on his face, he noticed.

I shook my head and clicked my tongue in aggravation. "Listen, Dominic. I wouldn't have asked you if I didn't want you to go. I want you to meet Vitto, and this is when he'll be available since he's so busy with interviews. He scheduled a whole bunch of them in a small amount of time." I bent down to fasten the strap on my teal suede pumps, and I could see from the corner of my eye that he didn't move right away. Straightening up, I found him standing there, watching me with an unreadable expression that made me feel self-conscious. I looked down at myself and then back up at him. "What? What's wrong? Does this outfit look bad?" I had on a matching teal top that hung off one shoulder and a pair of black skinny jeans.

Dominic moved to take a step forward and stopped. Instead, he placed his hands in his pockets and said, "Mia." He paused, closing his eyes. Opening them again, he stuttered, "You look amazing. I mean, you always do, but this is just . . . yeah. Amazing."

I felt the fire spread across my face and knew my cheeks were turning pink. Looking him right in the eyes but feeling embarrassed, I said, "Thank you." Then I remembered we had to go soon. "Now get going. We're going to be late." I laughed.

We went to Stick-n-Stein in El Segundo for a few beers and dinner. Vitto told Dominic all of my most embarrassing stories—or at least the ones he knew.

"So, she thought she could hang with the boys all the time. I swear it was wicked annoying. All the kids on the street knew about the fort we had made underneath the porch of one of the neighbor's houses." His accent was so strong, his "I sweah" and "neighbahs" sticking out noisily.

"Somehow she heard that we were going to the center to hang out. We were meeting girls there, and she wanted to go. We all told her no, but she would have followed us anyway because she was a frickin' brat. I had to come up with a way to get rid of her, so I told her we were all meeting at the fort and she should go wait for us there and we'd take her."

Vitto took a sip of his beer, then ran his hand over his hair down to his mullet tail, holding it in a ponytail for a moment. Most of us had brown hair with brown eyes, and Vitto was no exception. He wasn't that tall, though—about five-six. Although he was still stuck in the eighties, he owned it. Confidence rolled off him in waves.

Dominic looked confused and asked, "What's the center?"

I laughed a little. "Oh, that's the center of town. That's where all the stores were. The CVS, McDonald's, the grocery store, and a few more businesses," I answered, and he nodded.

Vitto continued. "Man, she was wicked excited and ran over to the fort and waited for hours." His guffaws were growing louder, and he was beginning to attract attention. "We had been to the center and back when my aunt called my house looking for her. She said she hadn't seen Mia all day, and it was dark out already. I ran out of the house to the fort, and sure enough, she was still there, knocked out. When I woke her up, she was pissed. Didn't talk to me for days after that." Vitto's hands were flying around while he told his story. Like a typical Italian storyteller, his voice got louder and louder as he spoke. I loved it and had missed the exciting conversations with my family.

The three of us had a great time; it was nice to go out and have some adult interaction. It was something I felt like I hadn't done in years, not to mention spending time with Vitto—that was always important to me, since I didn't have much family there.

I begged Vitto to come back for Christmas if he could. With luck, he would get a job soon and be living here by then. I was just starting to look forward to the holidays coming up. Dominic and I could take Lucia trick-or-treating, cook dinner for Thanksgiving, open gifts in front of the tree, and ring in the New Year together. Lucia and I had never shared those things with anyone else except for my dad. It had been just the two of us. Alex always seemed to have an emergency every single holiday, and he'd rushed to the office before we were even awake. It sounded ridiculous now; I couldn't imagine myself living in a relationship like that, but I had. I had become complacent and let things go.

Well, not this time, I promised myself. If I were to get involved with Dominic, I would never allow myself to take things for granted again. I was getting ahead of myself, but I knew that with time we'd be a couple. He might be picturing us together, too. Thinking of everything he did for us, it was easy to see how much he cared. He was amazing and genuine inside and out.

ॐ ॐ ॐ ॐ

Vitto called to tell me he would be in town for a few more days because he had a second interview scheduled with one of the businesses he had visited. Dominic and I decided to invite everyone over for a barbecue while Vitto was still available. I figured it would be a good idea for him to meet some of my friends since it was possible he would be living here soon.

Dominic, Vitto, and Gary were out on the balcony cooking, while Susan, Danielle, and I were surrounding the breakfast bar. Susan seemed distracted, and I watched her while she kept her attention on Vitto. I thought her interest in my cousin was a fascinating discovery and hoped the two could get to know each other better. Elbowing her side, I asked, "What ya looking at?" Payback was a bitch, so I teased her like she did me. "Either you're stuck on stupid, or you're watching my cousin out there."

Her freckled face lit up bright red. I knew that I blushed occasionally, but her cheeks turned red at the drop of a hat. Immediately, she snapped out of her embarrassment and had me laughing hard.

"Mia, where in the world have you been hiding him? I've known you for … what? Nine years, and you've never introduced us? I'm not sure I can forgive you for this."

I whacked her arm. "You'll forgive me soon. I'm not worried. Well, he's single and might move here. You should go talk to him. He's so easygoing, he'll be able to deal with your sassy mouth."

When I looked out the balcony doors to search for Dominic, he turned and looked me right in the eyes. He winked and took a swig from his beer before turning back to his conversation with the guys. That was new. He typically showed affection in everything he did for me, like how he'd warm my towels while I was in the shower, take my car for a wash and fill it with gas, and pick up all of my favorite products without being asked. There had been no specific declarations— but that wink was progress.

Later that night after everyone left, Dominic and I were both exhausted and a bit tipsy. We headed to our rooms, but Dominic grabbed my wrist before we parted ways. I stopped and looked up into his eyes. Even in the dark, I could see them sparkle. Thinking, hoping, and wishing he was going to kiss me, I held my breath in suspense. I wanted nothing more than to feel his soft lips touch mine.

I felt the goose bumps rise on my skin when he skimmed his hand up my arm. Closing my eyes to appreciate every single sensation, I lost myself in the moment without any other distractions. He was so close that I could feel his warm breath against my forehead. The feeling of his fingernails grazing my skin up to my jaw left me feeling faint. Still hoping he would bend down and kiss me, I stood there waiting, as patient as I could be. Before I knew it, however, his hand was gone from my face, and I was left with just the lingering sensation of his thumb making its way over my lips. I was a hot mess after that, and very disappointed that he hadn't kissed me.

Chapter 15
Catch and Kiss

Dominic had been giving me flirtatious looks and touching me a lot more. He would run his hand along my shoulder when he made his way to his chair in the dining room, or touch my hand a bit longer than normal when we passed each other something across the table. I would catch him staring at me from a distance, and I imagined he was watching me to see if he could catch me watching him in return.

There was a desire deep inside me to spend every single moment I could in his presence. I wanted to get home from work each night in time to help him cook dinner. It was an intimate task, and in my small galley kitchen, we couldn't help bumping into each other.

One night, we were making spaghetti, and I was stirring my homemade sauce at the stove. I removed the wooden spoon from the pot so I could grab some paper towels from under the sink. I didn't see Dominic behind me, and my spoon hit him straight on the ass, leaving a big splotch of sauce. He looked back over his shoulder, completely shocked. I began laughing, first at the mishap and then at the look on his face, and I couldn't stop.

Bent over gasping for breath, I felt him run a line of sauce from my forehead down to the tip of my nose with a spoon. I stood straight up in shock.

"Oh, my God! I can't believe you did that!" I shrieked.

In between breaths, he wheezed out, "Hey, you got me first," and pointed to his ass.

"Yeah, but that was an accident," I choked out between the belly laughs that were wracking my body.

We were both laughing so loudly that Lucia came in to see what was happening with a face full of wonderment. "What are you guys doing?" she asked.

Dominic and I looked at each other, and then another round of laughter poured from us.

When she didn't receive an answer, Lucia just huffed in exasperation and stormed out of the room.

Dominic was so easy to spend time with. He was kind and giving, and I hoped that I would never take advantage of that. I needed to figure out how to always remember that his kindness was a gift. Women took advantage of nice men all the time. I was sure he would keep me grounded, and, when needed, he could put me in my place.

Part of our new routine was ending the day with conversation and a movie, and it seemed we were both anxious to put Lucia to bed at eight so we could get to it. We began to get to know each other better since we had time to speak without interruption. The first night we talked, I told him more about my childhood and about growing up in Boston.

"Tell me one thing you liked about living there that you miss."

That was an easy question to answer.

"The biggest one was being surrounded by my family. I had my aunt and uncle next door with my six cousins, and I spent all of my spare time with them. When I moved here it was just my father and me."

I hated saying that out loud and sounding like I was looking for pity. Although it hadn't been my choice, I thought I did pretty well on my own at the time. "I always wanted to have a big brood of my own. I hope someday I can give Lucia many brothers and sisters," I said wistfully.

He held my hand and squeezed. "You will," Dominic said with conviction.

The next night, we settled down with popcorn and *A Beautiful Life*, which I thought was a wonderful movie even though it felt slow.

"It's my turn to ask a question." Turning to face him on the sofa I ran my hand down his arm to draw his attention to the natural bronze color of his skin. "What nationality are you?" I had to ask, because I was always interested in the origin of things and people.

"That's it? That's an easy one. Okay, let's see . . . My father's family is English, hence my English name. In fact, I'm named after him. I'm Dominic Roberts, Jr," he said with pride. "But my mother is Greek with a little French thrown in. You'll see when you meet her that her skin is like mine and my brother's. My mother's father was born in Greece, and her maiden name was Panas."

"Wow, no wonder you're so beautiful. What are your parents and grandparents like?" I asked with honest curiosity before my face pinked up at my outburst.

He shook his head in amusement and sat up straighter to finish telling me about his family. "I don't remember my grandparents at all since they died when I was young. But my parents are . . . I don't know . . . I'd say they are prim and proper but down-to-earth, if that makes sense. I mean, they run in high society circles and always pushed us to excel in college and life, but when I decided to change my career, they were behind me all the way. They were so supportive and never tried to change my mind. I respect them for that and am very lucky to have them," he said with a faraway look on his face. I knew he must miss them.

Each night that passed, I noticed we would sit closer and closer together on the sofa, and Dominic's arm would end up behind me when it rested on the back of the couch.

One night, we watched one of my all-time favorite movies, *The Notebook*, which Dominic admitted to never having seen. When it ended, I looked over at him and saw him place his forefinger and thumb under each eye trying to hold in the tears. I thought it was funny that he didn't want me to see how much it affected him. Even though I wanted to tease him about it, I was touched that he felt secure enough to cry. It showed how big his heart was, and I cared for him even more because of it. But he still deserved to get busted.

"Aww, are you crying?" I teased.

He pulled his hand down and I bumped him with my shoulder.

"No!" he said a bit too fast.

I laughed, wanting to tease him a little. "Come on. It's okay. Real men cry, too."

He huffed and began tickling me. "I wasn't. My eyes were itchy, and I didn't want to rub them. That always makes it worse."

Shrieks escaped me at that point because he began tickling me. I begged and pleaded for him to stop, but he wouldn't relent. I squirmed and pushed him away, but he was too strong, so I used the oldest trick in the book. "Stop, please! I have to pee! I don't want to pee on you," I panted, out of breath.

Dominic stopped right away, but I didn't attempt to move. His hands gripped my sides.

"You're such a faker, Mia. You don't play fair."

"Never said I did."

We looked at each other for a long moment, and then his mouth connected with mine. His lips were unsure at first, and I responded in an instant. My hands went to his shoulders and caressed his neck. I dug my fingers into the layers of hair and down to his shoulders, making short circuits up and down. Dominic's hands slid up my sides to my neck and face. With his thumbs, he caressed my cheeks, and I pulled back, looking into his hooded and glistening eyes and seeing such sincerity there. The tips of his fingers wove their way into my hair. I loved the way he held my face with such reverence and gentleness.

Our lips touched again, and I felt his tongue against mine. He tasted sweet and salty from the soda and popcorn. I nibbled his bottom lip, and he yelped a bit when he felt my teeth.

Just as I slid my hands down his back, he broke the kiss. He still held my face and looked into my eyes, straight to my soul.

"I've been wanting to do that for so long." He placed his forehead against mine as he held my gaze.

"Why didn't you?" I asked in a breathy whisper.

He kissed my lips again and sat back. His fingers slid down my arms until they reached my hands, which he then squeezed. "For many reasons. First, this was supposed to be just a job — a job I wanted very much. It was going to be the gateway to the big life change I was trying to accomplish. And I didn't want to cross the line, but in all honesty, you never made me feel like just an employee. Second, I wanted to get to know you better, to bond with you. Third, I wanted to make sure my feelings would be welcomed by you, and if they weren't, that it wouldn't affect Lucia."

I told him my honest feelings, even though I was sure he would think I was crazy. "I felt something for you the moment we met." I laughed a little because I was sure he already knew that. "I knew it would be so easy to fall in love with you someday. I had no idea if you felt anything because you remained so indifferent."

Dominic shook his head. "No, Mia. I wasn't indifferent. I tried to hide my attraction from you. I didn't want you to think I just wanted this job so I could have an instant family, although, with you and Lucia, that was all I wanted from day one. You both made your way into my heart, and I have all these feelings for you two."

I just sat there gaping at him, in shock that he had said those words—and before I had! He was more reserved than me, so I always thought that, if that moment ever came, I would have to coax the admission out of him.

He panicked a bit, and I could see stress lines forming on his forehead again. "It's too soon, isn't it? I mean, to talk about feelings and stuff. I don't want to ruin this. I don't want to scare you off."

"No, you can't scare me off. I'm just surprised because I didn't think you felt that much for me. Don't worry; I've felt something from the moment you walked in that door. I've wanted to spend every possible moment with you since then." I squeezed his hands tighter to stress the sincerity of my words. "I may have been falling in love with you since the day we met. You have made your way into our hearts as well. My daughter looks to you as a father figure, something she's never had. We're a package deal, and you've cared for and loved us in your own special way since you arrived."

I thought about every little nice thing he'd done for me—for us. The lunches he would pack for us with a little note wishing us a good day. The way he would ensure I had fresh warm towels after my shower, and how my bed was always made. The way he would explain Lucia's homework to her like the most patient man in the world and brush the tangles out of her hair at night with such gentleness it swelled my heart. She deserved the love of a father.

"I just didn't want to put myself out there. Even though I may come off as confident, I'm afraid of rejection," I said, wondering how I was able to talk about this so easily with him. He was still anxious, and I wanted to give him the security of his place here in our lives. "You've belonged with us since the day you arrived. You fit right in without a single hiccup. It was like we were all meant to be together."

Dominic's smile brightened when he registered what I'd said. "I would like us to become a family," he said with sincerity.

I nodded and said, "I'd like that, too. We just need to take it slow, okay? I'm a little gun shy."

"Me too, but what we have between us is so different and special, we'll make it work."

Chapter 16
Ring around the Rosy

I was overwhelmed by the beautiful scent of roses, lavender, and jasmine that surrounded us. In the middle of the park sat metal structures in the forms of monkey bars, swings, and a gigantic slide. Dominic was pushing Lucia on the swings while I sat on the bench near them. It was a beautiful, warm, October day and I was enjoying the heat of the sun. It seemed like other parents had the same idea, because they were also running around the park with their children.

Lucia jumped from the swing and, to my great relief, landed on her two little feet. She gestured to Dominic in an excited manner, and they both ran toward me. I sat up straighter and felt the smile spread across my face. Holding my arms out and open, ready to catch her when she jumped in them, I hugged her to me. However, she backed away and shouted out, "Come on, Momma. Let's go to the slide. I want you to go down with me."

I looked over at the monstrosity she called a slide and weighed my options. Praying that I'd make it down safe and sound, I agreed and began the climb with her. Once we got to the top, she sat down and waited for me to sit. I placed her between my legs and held her around the waist before whispering in her ear, "Are you ready?"

She clapped. "Yup, I'm ready!" And with her last word, I scooted forward, and we went flying down, right into Dominic's waiting arms.

Things with Dominic had been moving along since that night we expressed our feelings for each other. Although our physical relationship hadn't gone beyond kissing and heavy petting, he had picked up his game. I was a big ball of sexual tension.

Strong arms wrapped around Lucia and me, and the feel of him supporting both of us made me feel safe and loved.

Looking over his shoulder, I could see several women speed-walking around the edge of the park for their daily exercise and others just strolled as they gossiped with their friends. The idea of a stroll around the park sounded good.

"You guys want to take a walk with me?" I asked.

Dominic looked down at Lucia once he'd placed her back on the ground and asked, "What do you think?"

"Sure, but I want you both to hold my hands," she said as she shrugged her shoulders.

With Lucia in the middle, swinging back and forth, we went off on a stroll together. Polite nods and a few hellos to the folks we passed and Lucia's squeals accompanied us halfway around the park.

"Lucia, hold on tight so we can do a big one," Dominic said. I braced myself, squeezed her hand, and swung her so high, her white tennis shoes were almost at eye level. And that's when I noticed the couple walking toward us. In complete shock, I almost let go of Lucia's hand. My feet stopped without conscious thought, and I stood there, frozen. Dominic and Lucia were jerked back by my sudden halt. Out of the corner of my eye, I could see Dominic looking at me questioningly, but I couldn't tear my attention away from the sight in front of me to explain to him.

I stared, unnoticed for the moment, when he caressed the woman's rounded belly while they strolled carefree through the park. They were a few feet in front of me but had not looked up yet. There was no escape for me, so I just stood, waiting for him to notice. It felt like it took years for them to reach us. When he looked up, he paled. Yeah, I knew the feeling. I had hoped never to see him again.

"Mia . . . Uh, hi. Um . . . how are you?" Alex asked, sputtering with nerves. His eyes lingered over Lucia, and then glanced at Dominic. I didn't want Alex to see my daughter, since he had no right to, so I stepped to my right and covered her a bit. She peeked out, though, sneaking looks at them. I could tell that Dominic had figured out who this man was, because he took a stance in front of Lucia and me, just off to my right. Alex looked affronted at that movement and scoffed visibly. *Asshole!*

I took a deep, cleansing breath and called forth all of my confidence. "Oh, wow! Hi, you two." My voice came out in a much higher tone than usual. "Don't you look wonderful," I said, when I pointed toward the girl on Alex's arm. It was the same girl I had seen in his office bathroom the night I caught him.

The girl's hands covered her stomach in a protective manner, and she and Alex just stood there, waiting for me to snap. I wasn't upset at seeing them together; I'd just never wanted Lucia to see him again and ask me questions. How could I tell my baby girl that her biological father never wanted her, never loved her, yet had a new baby on the way?

"This is my boyfriend, Dominic. And this is Alex and . . . what's your name? Sorry, I didn't catch it when we met in the bathroom."

She didn't answer, but Alex did. "It's nice to meet you, man. This is Amber, my wife."

And that was all it took. "Well, Amber, if you're lucky, all that love and attention he's showing you now won't end the moment your baby is born, like it did with us. I hope he won't do to you what he did to us, for your child's sake—"

"That's enough, Mia," Alex interrupted.

I nodded, shaking with anger. "You're right. It *is* enough." Reaching for Lucia's hand, I walked away.

I was nearly at our car when Dominic caught up to us. He was talking to me, but I didn't register what he was saying. I was so angry that I was caught in the maelstrom of my mind until Lucia screamed and I felt Dominic's hand on mine, trying to stop me.

"Momma, you're hurting me." Lucia began to cry, and I realized I had been walking too fast and held her hand too tight

Snapping out of it, I stopped dead in my tracks, and the tears began to fall. "Oh, God," I breathed. "I'm so sorry." Looking into Dominic's eyes, I pleaded, "Please take me home."

Swooping Lucia into one arm, and then wrapping the other around me for support, he guided us to the car. Lucia was still crying. I had scared her with my actions, and she was confused. I knew she would have a ton of questions later after we had all settled down.

Lucia fell asleep in the car, and I just stared out the side window, wondering how Alex could replace us so easily. It was as if we had never existed. I didn't love him—I knew that to be true—but seeing him after all this time brought up the feelings I had never dealt with when he walked away from us without a second glance.

Upon entering the house, Dominic took Lucia straight to her room. I didn't know what to do with myself, so I remained in the entryway, just waiting for something, anything. I felt hurt, betrayed, and just plain drained. Before I even realized what was happening, Dominic had lifted me up and carried me to my bed. Removing my shoes he said, "Why don't you take a nap? You'll feel better."

"Will you stay with me? I don't want to be alone."

After slipping off his own shoes, he laid down next to me. His comforting arms circled me and pulled me toward him to spoon me, and I wrapped my hand around his where it lay across my ribcage. I felt his warm breath on my neck, and then felt the vibration of his words. "Do you want to talk about it?"

I sighed, letting out a deep breath. "I feel so many things, Dominic. I just don't know what it all means."

Dominic pulled his hand from mine and pushed the hair off my face. He turned my face toward him a bit so he could look me in the eyes. "Tell me."

That simple request opened the floodgates. Feeling the tears dripping down my face into my ears, I heard myself speak as if it were someone else. Things I had not even thought about spilled from my mouth.

"He hurt me and betrayed me for God knows how long. In all honesty, I thought it didn't matter. I thought I was okay with it because I had Lucia and I had to protect her. Not once did I feel this pain." Rolling over to look at him better, I kept trying to explain. I wanted him to understand; *I* wanted to understand. It seemed as if the words were flowing from my mouth without my permission.

"It's not that I still love him, because I don't at all. But, wow, what a rejection. I mean, he just discarded and replaced us like we were nothing. Caring for our home, our child, and him—despite the fact that he was never there and didn't reciprocate for years—wasn't enough? How does that reflect on me? All these insecurities that I didn't think I had are coming up for me now." I sat up in a panic. "God, I think I compartmentalized it all. I never gave much thought as to why it was so easy for him to replace me. My whole life was a lie, and I let it be that. And God knows for how long. I ignored the fact that he was never home yet I blame him for it all when I was just as responsible."

My breaths were coming in short pants and my head felt dizzy. I didn't know what was wrong with me. Why didn't I ever say anything to Alex? I never forced the issue of him being gone all the time until the very end. For five years, I played single mother and thought I was happier that way. What if I was not capable of a relationship? What if I screwed this up with Dominic?

He turned me toward him, placed my hand on his chest, and spoke in soothing tones, "Listen . . . Take a deep breath, in and out. That's it, baby. Slow. In and out."

I felt his chest rise and fall under my palm. When I matched my breathing to his, it went back to normal. My eyes were focused solely on his. Those beautiful green orbs were soft and concerned.

"Mia, what happened between you and Alex is . . . well, it was just meant to happen that way. It was to give you Lucia, because without her, we would have never met." Dominic looked at me with love and sincerity. "We were meant to happen. Lucia was meant to happen. So, without that jackass, we would have never found each other. Just think what a tragedy that would have been. And, listen, you have to stop beating yourself up over this. Yes, you were complacent. Yes, you had a part in the failure of the marriage, but he was already doing what he was doing. You just let it happen. You didn't love him, so it was easy to let him go. And that's what you did when he stopped coming home. At least you understand it all now." Holding my face in his hands and swiping my tears with his thumbs, he peppered my eyes with small, reverent kisses.

I kept my lids closed and left my hand on his chest, counting his breaths. "You're right," I said, "I didn't fight for him, and I let him go the minute he checked out emotionally. I'm not even sure I know how to love. Being able to give my all to Lucia from day one and to never think of Alex was too easy. What does that mean? Why didn't it bother me until it was too late? What if I'm not capable of being in a healthy relationship because I . . . I don't know. What if I'm not good at it, and you regret us?" I was so confused. So many things were running through my mind. "I just hope that things work out better for his new wife and baby, because it would be a shame for another child to be left fatherless by him," I said with sadness in my voice.

"Lucia is not fatherless."

With those words, my eyes flipped open and faced his, which were full of conviction. Once the words sunk in, I jumped toward him and wrapped my arms around his neck, hugging him with enough force to let him know how much his words meant to me. My heart clenched; it hurt, but it was a good kind of pain. Dominic was the most kind-hearted man I had ever met.

"Well, she's going to have questions when she wakes. I'm sure she recognized him. I mean, she's seen pictures, and he was around every now and again. "

"We'll do this together," Dominic said firmly. "Whatever questions she has, we'll answer as best we can."

I nodded.

And she did have questions, but not the ones I thought she would. Lucia mainly wanted to know why I had been upset enough to hurt her. After I explained that I didn't mean to cause her pain and had just wanted to get out of there, she went on to her next question with all the brusque charm of a six year old.

"So, that man was my dad," she said, more a statement than a question.

How would I explain this to her? "Lucia, he was your father. He helped me make you, but he was never your daddy. He never took you to play at the park, to a ballet class, or ever picked you up from school. A daddy is someone who takes care of you and is there for you, and a father just makes you. Does that make sense?" The term sperm donor came to mind but there was no way I could explain that to Lucia.

Her little head tilted to the side in concentration. I knew she was trying to piece it all together. "So, does that mean Dominic is my daddy? He does all those things."

This girl was going to be the death of me; she was too smart for her own good.

"No, he's not your daddy. We are working toward it. You see all the hard work Dominic has been doing to learn how to do all of those things with you, right? We all want nothing more than for him to be your daddy, and we'll get there soon, I promise. Okay?"

She looked at us, not quite convinced, but I had no idea how to explain it further. The truth was, Dominic and I were just starting a relationship. I couldn't let Lucia believe he was her daddy, and then have something go wrong between us. Our relationship had to progress in its own time and couldn't be rushed just because of what Lucia wanted. However, I did believe, in my heart, that Dominic wanted to be called Lucia's daddy more than anything in the world.

Chapter 17
Chopsticks

Two weeks before Halloween, Dominic, Lucia and I were standing in Party City staring at a long wall of costumes. There were too many options, and Lucia was overwhelmed with them all. The girls' side alone took up half the wall.

I was beginning to crawl out of my skin with impatience. We had been standing there for over thirty minutes, and we weren't one step closer to finding a costume. Dominic, forever the patient man, was caught up in the excitement of all the choices and the holiday itself.

"Do you want to be a Disney princess or a super hero? Or wait, look at those Monster High costumes!" he exclaimed, a bit glassy-eyed while he examined the huge selection.

"I like Cinderella because she's so pretty and . . . what's the word, Momma? Classic?" Lucia looked at me for confirmation, and I nodded. "But my favorite is Tinkerbell. She looks like a ballerina, and her costume matches Dominic's eyes."

My head snapped up to look at her and then over to Dominic, and I couldn't help smiling. I couldn't believe the things my kid said sometimes. Dominic was hiding his amusement because he didn't want to embarrass Lucia, but I could tell he found it amusing and maybe even a bit flattering.

Suddenly I realized she had made a decision, and I jumped all over it. "So, you want the Tinkerbell costume?" I asked while reaching to take it off the hook on the wall.

"Yeah, I think so."

I sighed in frustration. "You need to be sure, Lucia. I don't want us to get home and have you decide that wasn't what you wanted. Whatever you pick today is it. Okay?" With the costume in one hand, I ran the other through my hair while I prayed she would just choose a costume so we could go. I was hungry and tired and feeling grouchy.

Watching my struggle, Dominic jumped in after he flashed me a "calm down" look. He knelt down at Lucia's level, leaning on one knee while he ran his hand down her arm to soothe her. "I think you've made a wonderful choice. Her green dress and slippers do look like a ballet costume, and with your hair up in a bun, you will look like a fairy ballerina. And I think the most special thing about it is that you think the outfit matches my eyes. That's very sweet."

She looked up at him in awe and amazement. I could see she was losing the battle and was submitting to his convincing words. "Yeah, she's my favorite." Then, turning to look at me, she said, "I want Tinkerbell, Momma. Let's go." She looked back at Dominic, reached for his hand, and led him to the front of the store, with me following behind. Always the gentleman, Dominic looked over his shoulder and reached for my hand as well.

వా వా యా యా

Halloween was fast approaching, but, in typical Los Angeles fashion, there were no natural telltale signs. The leaves didn't change color, the sun shone, kids were running around without jackets, and people barbecued. The weather was still quite hot, and it made for a nice night since most kids would be trick-or-treating in very thin costumes.

Dominic continued to take care of both Lucia and me every day without a single complaint. Lucia told me how he calmed her when she started to get worked up over her upcoming ballet recital. He practiced creating the bun on Lucia's head over and over so he could get it right without hurting her. The patience he showed when teaching her how to cook, how to ride her bike, and practicing her ballet positions was heartwarming. He was the perfect man, if there ever was one, but I still couldn't let my heart commit all the way. I was looking for flaws. No one could be perfect. I knew I was a lot to deal with, but he handled me just fine. And even though he did all of those great things for us, he was still a very particular man. Our home was now arranged to his liking, and he hated it when we moved something and he couldn't find it. Placing his cooking utensils in the wrong drawer in the kitchen would be enough to cause a fight in about two seconds. I didn't complain but it showed his controlling nature and I supposed that could be considered a flaw.

I arrived home one evening after work to find my two favorite people giggling on the living room floor. Upon opening the door, the first things I heard were Lucia's squealing laughs and Dominic's deep chuckles echoing through our home. He was sitting against the sofa with his knees up in a pair of gray sweats and a black T-shirt. Lucia was bent over in front of him with a bottle of nail polish in her hand, painting his toenails. They looked up at the sound of the door closing and saw me standing there with tears in my eyes and a grand smile on my face. Dominic's ears pinked, as they always did when he'd been caught doing something cute. I dropped my purse on the bar and walked over to them to peek at Lucia's masterpiece.

"Wow, Lucia. Nice work," I exclaimed at the black toenails with pink polka dots—dots that had bled into blobs. I could tell she used the brush to create them. Looking into Dominic's beautiful eyes, I mouthed, "Thank you."

He dismissed it with a quick shrug. He had told me a million times to stop thanking him for doing things with Lucia that he wanted to do. "Welcome home," Dominic said with his hands resting on his knees. He was relaxed and seemed to be having a good time.

"So, what's the occasion?" I asked, pointing at his toes.

"Momma, I'm practicing how to paint nails nice and do designs like you get on your toes from the salon. Maybe I can do yours when I get good." Lucia looked up at me with proud eyes. She screwed the cap back onto the bottle and placed it on the towel under Dominic's feet.

He had wanted us to have a serious conversation with Lucia about our new boyfriend/girlfriend status, but I didn't think we needed an official conversation. I figured she'd get the picture through our actions. We were holding hands, hugging, and playing around a bit more, but we hadn't kissed in front of her yet. I was sure the moment we did, she would get the idea, but he thought it was important to speak with her about our developing relationship. Unsure of what to say, myself, I figured I would just follow Dominic's lead.

I gave a subtle gesture to ask if he wanted to talk then and he nodded.

"Lucia, why don't you put that stuff away, and then come back? We want to talk to you for a moment, okay?" I helped her pick up the bottles of polish while Dominic sat on the sofa so she could grab the towel and put everything away.

I looked at Dominic with questioning eyes, and he nodded. "You're going to tell her, right?"

He nodded again, laughing at my nervousness.

I sat, waiting for Lucia to come back, bouncing my leg up and down in anxiety. She ran in happily, not sensing my stress in the least. Dominic sat next to me, leaning back with his fingers woven behind his head in complete comfort. Lucia planted herself between us and asked, "What is it?" Ever so blunt, just like her mother.

I cut my eyes to Dominic and arched my brow, waiting for him to begin his speech.

"Lucia, your mom and I want to talk to you about us," he said waggling his finger between the three of us. "Your mom and I want to be a couple–" He stopped because of the look of confusion on Lucia's face. Her face was contorted, eyebrows scrunched together, mouth closed in a crooked line, and her nose wrinkled up a bit. She was too cute.

"A what?" she asked.

"Boyfriend and girlfriend," I answered this time.

"Pfft. I knew that already."

It was our turn to look confused. "What? How?" I asked.

"Momma, get serious! You guys hug and hold hands a lot. Isn't that was you do with a boyfriend?"

I was right; this conversation wasn't needed. "So, are you okay with it? I mean, you're not upset or anything?"

She scoffed. "No! I think it's cool. It will make us a family quicker, and then Dominic can be my daddy."

My eyebrows went sky high, and I thought I was going to faint. I looked at Dominic to finish the conversation because I was at a loss. She was too smart for her own good, and I had a feeling that we would soon be a unit in one way or another. It might not be through legal channels such as marriage or adoption, but at least the commitment would be there.

"Come here, baby." Dominic opened his arms for her to climb onto his lap. "I don't want you to worry your pretty little head about anything, okay?"

"Momma, come look."

I made my way to Lucia's room and found her dressed in her Tinkerbell costume, with her hair done just like that adorable Disney character. I was in awe of Dominic's work. Her bangs were swept to the side of her forehead instead of slicked back as usual, and her bun was big on the top of her head. My hands went to my mouth to stifle the sob that wanted to escape. Every time Lucia was able to experience a daddy/daughter moment, I was overwhelmed and touched. Lucia had never before had what normal kids had with their fathers, and now that she did, I was so happy for her.

Moments like these reminded me of all I that I had missed growing up. Yes, I had a dad, but he hadn't been there for those everyday things. He never made it to my dance recitals or school plays. He wasn't able to take pictures with me for my first dance. I didn't have memories of him taking care of me when I was sick or needed him around. He lived out of state and only acted a father when I visited him. I had no doubt, now that I was an adult, that he loved me and would have done anything for me, but it was the small, day-to-day things I'd missed.

I wanted more than anything in the world for my baby girl to have it all. Her father figure might have arrived a bit late, but better late than never. She deserved this and so much more. Dominic was going to be here for her, and he would show her what a father did and was. I chuckled, thinking about how she might not appreciate it so much when she began dating and he chased all her suitors away, but at least she could know she would have him there for her when she eventually came home with a broken heart.

"Are you okay?" I felt Dominic's hands caressing my face, wiping away the tears that fell from my eyes.

Looking up at him, I answered, "I am. More than okay. You just don't know how much this touches me," I whispered, gesturing toward Lucia, who was checking herself out in the full-length mirror hanging on her closet door.

"I know, because it means a lot to me, too." His lips touched mine, feather soft, while he held my face protected in the palms of his loving hands.

The moment ended much too soon when Lucia asked if it was time to go trick-or-treating.

"Well, look out the window and see if it's dark yet."

Lucia ran to the window and stood on her tiptoes to peek out. "It is, Momma. It's dark. Let's go!" She grabbed our hands and walked us to the door.

"Okay, hold on. Let me turn off the lights and get the keys."

We walked all through the community to as many of the homes as we could. The small streets in our secured community were filled with tons of children running around, yelling, and examining their candy. The excitement that vibrated off the kids was contagious. Lucia was beautiful in her costume, and I hadn't seen any other kids dressed like Tinkerbell, so it was a winning situation for her. Dominic insisted on walking her to every door, even though she already had three bags of candy. When I teased him about it and reminded him that part of the fun of the night was to watch the kids walk up to the door alone or in a group of other kids, he wouldn't hear of it.

"Let me be. I haven't done this since I was a kid and never as the parental figure. I want to enjoy it," he chided while he wrapped his arms around me from behind and kissed my neck. Chills broke out through my body while he learned where all my sensitive spots were.

"Okay, okay. The night's all yours. Go and enjoy while you can, because it's possible next year she won't even want to be seen with us," I teased.

We walked hand-in-hand back to our home, each of us carrying a bag full of her candy. After we sorted it, I'd have to make some of it disappear, or else she would eat every single piece.

I looked at Dominic once we were seated around the bar to go through the candy.

"This was a lot of fun. I'm so glad we could do this together," I said.

"Me, too. I wouldn't trade this for anything in the world."

Chapter 18
Follow the Leader

Settled on the sofa after Lucia was bathed and tucked in, we got ready for our movie. We had begun to choose slow, boring films so we wouldn't get sucked in. Instead, we'd sit, talk, and grope like teenagers.

"Dominic, babe. When you come with the popcorn, can you bring me a beer, please?"

I watched him work his way around the kitchen, popping popcorn, pulling out bowls, and getting our beers. He ended up choosing the big bowl and dumping all of the popcorn in there so we could share. It was always better that way because our hands met at the bottom of the bowl. When he walked toward me, something from inside told me it was time to tell him how I felt about him.

He placed the bowl on the table and pushed one of the bottles of beer toward me. I met his eyes and thanked him. His olive colored skin was covered by day-old scruff, but the darkness of his stubble contrasted with his bright, beautiful, green eyes, which shined like polished apples. The fullness of his lips made them look so delicious when he smiled that he always managed to take my breath away.

Dominic and I sat close together, and he put his arm around me. From the crook of his arm, I looked up at his breathtaking face. I didn't feel close enough to him; I wanted to climb onto him — into him. Just . . . closer. He looked down at me, and I knew it was the right moment.

"Baby, I, uh . . ." My heart began beating triple time. The words were on the tip of my tongue but wouldn't come out.

"What is it? What's wrong?" Concerned, Dominic wrapped his hand around mine and squeezed.

"I just want you to know how thankful I am for having you in my life. And I want to know how much I love you." My voice cracked. I sat there gazing into his eyes, waiting for a reaction. The nervousness bubbled inside me, and if he didn't say something soon, I was either going to laugh or cry. I was betting on crying.

I wasn't sure if I was sharing my feelings with Dominic too soon or not, but it made me feel like an emotional mess. I tended to feel everything so fiercely; it didn't matter the emotion, I wore my feelings on my sleeve for all to see and I'd release each one in an outburst. And then, after the outburst, I would wonder if I had overreacted because I had never been able to judge for myself. I felt an overwhelming love for Dominic, and I needed him to know. He was always so giving of himself that I wanted to give him something of me in return.

His hands cradled my face, and he looked deep into my eyes. Never had I spoken words so sincere, and he saw that.

"I love you, too. So very much." I felt the vibration of those loving words pitter-patter against my mouth. His eyes were closed tight when his lips touched mine once again. "Thank you," he cried, his voice cracking.

His hands went to my shoulders, and he pulled me close to him, wrapping me in an embrace. I buried my face in his chest and slid my arms around his back. Dominic crashed his lips to mine and kissed me with all he had. His hands wrapped around my head, cradling my skull as if he was afraid I would back away. I would never have considered it, so I matched his passion and then doubled it. I wrapped my hands around his shoulders, pulling him closer to me. No longer satisfied with the teenage groping we had been doing up to this point, I wanted us to consummate our relationship — to share and express our love in the ultimate way. I realized I didn't want to wait until I was married to take that step.

"Baby," I said against his lips, not willing to separate, "Let's go to my room."

He stopped and pulled back to look me in the eyes. "Are you sure?"

I smiled and pulled at the neck of his t-shirt with a crooked finger. "Yes. Let's go," I whispered.

೪ড়ড়৶৶

I had never seen this man undressed before. Standing in my room, feeling shy all of a sudden, I watched while he removed his clothes and unveiled his beauty. In all honesty, I didn't know what to expect. I had seen glimpses of him, small parts here and there, while we groped like kids on the sofa during our movie nights. When his shirt went over his head, I savored every toned muscle and found myself eager to touch every part of him. Anxiety ran through me while my eyes bounced over every bare piece of his skin. I felt the instant need to skim my fingers through the light scatter of hair on his chest that disappeared into his jeans. I wanted to taste the salt on his skin when I licked the "v" at his hips.

The confidence I had in the living room faded when we faced each other. I wanted to close the distance, to touch him, but my nerves set in. My mind was running with different, crazy thoughts. What if he didn't like my body? I had a baby, after all. What if he didn't find me experienced enough? What if I couldn't please him? I steeled myself and began to undress alongside him. My body shook with nerves and anticipation, and I couldn't wait to feel him. My body begged for fast and rough, but my heart yearned for soft and sensual.

"Whoa, not so fast, baby. I want to do that," he said in a playful tone that relaxed me and made me giggle.

Standing back, I watched when he let his pants drop to the floor so I was able to appreciate his strong legs. They were long, with defined muscles covered in black wisps of hair. He placed his pants on the chair behind him, and I caught a look at his tight ass in his dark gray boxer briefs. As a full package, Dominic was complete perfection. Hell, even in parts he was beautiful. When he turned back toward me, he looked right into my eyes, and I let out a shaky breath. My eyes were sucked in by his, and I watched while they changed color, turning darker. In the look we shared, our souls just spoke—*connected*. It was the kind of moment I had read about in fairy tales; it was not something that happened in real life, but it happened now. It happened for us.

"Come here." He held out his hand to me. "Let me love you."

Two quick steps, and I was in his arms with my face buried in his neck, which allowed me to smell his sweet, musky scent. Dominic was taking his time while he held me close, savoring every moment, and it just served to build up the anticipation. I could feel his heart beating fast in his chest, just as mine was. His skin felt soft over his firm muscles when I ran my hands down his back. Dancing up to my neck, his hand then trailed to my chin with the lightest touch of his fingertips. He lifted my face to look at him and closed his lips over mine. They were rough, and his mouth was filled with desire. The scruff from his light beard rubbed my skin, leaving it sensitive. The blood coursed through my body, pulsating through every inch of my skin that prickled from our connection. It was different from any kiss we had ever shared. It was desperate, promising, loving, committed, and exciting. Then, he trailed those emotion-filled kisses from my mouth down my chin to my neck, nipping and licking along the way.

His hands skimmed around my stomach, where he found the hem of my shirt and slid it up my body and over my head. Then he undid my jeans and wiggled them down over my hips, bending down to help me and throwing them on the chair with his own clothes.

Dominic walked me back to the bed and, with his hands under my ass, he lifted me on top of the comforter. His kisses stopped so he could remove my bra and panties, and he savored every surface of my body with his eyes. My tongue swiped my bottom lip, and I dragged it into my mouth, embedding my teeth into it. My chest rose and fell exaggeratedly while my breathing became shallow just from watching him devour me with his gaze.

Steam covered the windows like a thin shade. The light shone from the chandelier above us, and I saw the small beads of sweat drop from Dominic's forehead and chest as he moved over my body. While we kissed, touched, moved, and caressed, we shared every part of ourselves with each other.

When our eyes met again, his had darkened like uncut emeralds. His expression was ravenous, like a thirsty man in a desert. And when I looked deep into his eyes, swept up in our moment, thoughts of our first meeting came back to me. The connection I felt the moment we first touched rushed through me. The flashes I had of our future together were coming to fruition. We were sealing our fate while we connected in every possible way.

Dominic squeezed his eyes shut, snapping me back from the memories. He moaned with each movement, each caress. The weight of his body covered me like a heavy blanket on a cool night.

When my back arched and we set free, we collapsed on my sweat-soaked sheets.

"Wow!" I laughed in amazement. God, that had been incredible.

He chuckled with me. "I know."

Sated and wrapped around him, I couldn't help but think how much I loved this man with every part of my being: mind, body, heart, and soul.

My fingers ran across his sweaty face, over his eyebrows, around his eyes, and down the bridge of his nose to the tip. I made soothing circuits to his lips and traced around his jaw to lull him to sleep. I whispered, "I love you so much."

A smiled spread across his face and caused crinkles around his closed eyes. "I love you, too—so much." His arms tightened around me, and we fell deep into oblivion.

Chapter 19
Tiddlywinks

Waking up with Dominic wrapped around me for the first time was heaven. I was torn between wanting to stay in his arms to make love to him again and getting up to call Lori and tell her all about our connection the night before. I couldn't contain the excitement that was bubbling inside me; I was amazed with how everything just clicked.

Still, I worried about my abilities to love long-term and what would happen down the line when we got married and planned to have more children. Yes, I knew this would lead to marriage. Even though I wasn't sure when, I knew it would. I was only assuming he wanted children—at least I hoped he did, because there was nothing I wanted more. The biggest problem for me, though, was my fear of not being able to love Dominic with all the passion in the world forever – that another child would somehow steal that love away.

I rolled over to face Dominic, and he began to stir. While I watched him breathe, I took inventory of his precious face. His lashes were thick and short against his cheek. The stubble on his face had thickened a bit more, and his lips stuck out in a pout. I pecked them, and his eyes opened.

"Good morning, sleeping beauty," I said when he stretched and yawned. Dominic scratched at his stubble and rubbed his eyes. He was adorable in the morning.

"Mhmmm, it is a good morning," he said with a sleep-coated voice. He wrapped his arms around me and squeezed. "A very good morning."

"I need to get up and get ready for work. Lucia will be up in a bit. But . . ." I began to say.

"What's wrong?"

I exhaled a deep breath. "No, nothing's wrong, but, well, I really want you to move into my room now. Too soon?" I wasn't afraid he'd say no, but for some reason I felt strange about asking.

Dominic scoffed. "Did you think I was going to go back to sleeping in my room after that? It was the best night of my life," he said while peppering soft kisses on my face.

"It was my best night, too, baby." I kissed him and got up. "So, it's official then. You're moving in here, and we're a real couple." I jerked my head in a nod to emphasize my statement.

He rolled on top of me, pinning me down on the bed. "I thought it was a given, Mia. You're stuck with me forever now. I hope you can handle me," he said with a laugh.

"Mhmmm, I can handle you all right. I just hope you can handle *me*." I brushed his lips with mine. "Come on. I need to get up. I want to make you guys breakfast before I have to take Lucia to school, okay?"

I didn't have time to cook anything fancy, but I whipped up some scrambled eggs and fried some bacon. Next, I popped a few frozen waffles into the toaster and poured Lucia orange juice. Dropping in a K-cup of Dominic's favorite coffee, I added sugar to his mug before doing the same for myself.

When I ran down the hallway to Lucia's room, I heard Dominic singing Lucia a wake-up song. I'd had no idea he knew about that.

"Lucia, Lucia it's morning time, and if you get up, I'll give you a dime. Lucia, Lucia, stand on your feet, so we can go to the kitchen to sit down and eat," he sang in his deep voice. I watched from the doorway while he sat on the edge of her bed, stroking the hair off her face and singing. Although I didn't want to interrupt, the food was getting cold. I wanted to swoon over him paying attention to the made-up songs I had always sung to her in the morning, but I didn't want to embarrass him over it. Also, I was feeling a tad jealous. Those songs had always been my special connection with my daughter, but I knew I was lucky that he cared so much and was interested in being involved. Truthfully, he filled my heart to the rim.

"Hey, guys. The food's ready. Come on, Lucia, get up!" They both looked at me and laughed. "Hey, what's so funny?"

"Nothing, Momma." She sat up and jumped into Dominic arms, and he was quick enough to catch her.

♔ ♔ ♔ ♔

The day was beautiful. Well, it was overcast and foggy but it didn't affect me; I was way too giddy. All I felt was the happiness that spilled out of me when I remembered the wonderful time I'd had with Dominic the night before. So, I ignored the external gloom and rode to work on cloud nine.

My excitement was too much to keep inside. I needed to share it with someone. Since I wasn't close enough with Danielle to share the personal side of my relationship with her, I decided to call Lori.

Slipping in my Bluetooth earpiece, I dialed her number.

"Hey, girlie. How's it going?" Lori said with excitement in her voice.

"Hi, you busy?" I asked quickly.

"Nope, you caught me right at lunchtime."

I sighed in relief. "Oh, yeah, the time difference. Good. So . . ."

"So? So, what? What?" Her tone became more forceful. I was irritating her, and I loved it.

I drawled out again. "So. Guess what I did last night," I teased some more.

"Ugh, seriously, Mia. I'm going to fly there and kick your ass if you don't stop with your bullshit. Tell me!"

I laughed out loud at her, which I knew would only piss her off more.

"Take it easy there, killer. If you want me to share my secrets with you, you're going to have to be nice to me. *Capiche?*"

"Damn, Mia. I haven't heard you throw out any Italian in years. This must be good. I'll be nice. Now, spill." Demanding little brat.

I gave her a recap of the night before, leaving out the intimate details for privacy's sake.

"Wow, that's amazing," she said after I'd finished. "Congratulations, Mia."

"For what?" I asked.

"Well, for getting laid, for enjoying it, and for the great start to your relationship. But I have to ask: are you sure you're ready for this? You were both in serious relationships not that long ago, and I just want to make sure you're not jumping in too soon."

I thought about what she'd said for a moment. Despite having had same thoughts a million times before, I couldn't help but go with my instincts. With my marriage to Alex, I'd just jumped in and hadn't thought about anything at all. I never once dug deep down inside myself to see if I was in love with him or not. I just went with the flow, and when I got pregnant with Lucia, things just went a bit faster. Back then, I never questioned myself, but this time around, that's all I was doing. The answer was always the same.

"I am ready for this. I'm sure of it. And from what I know about Dominic, I think he is, too. He's just perfect for me, Lori. He loves my daughter as if she was his own, and he loves me as well. He shows us every day. It's like he knows what we need and he just . . . does it. He doesn't just spew a bunch of pretty words at me to make me feel nice. His actions speak much louder than his words ever could— though I have to tell you, he says some sweet-ass shit, too."

"Mia, if he's anything like his brother, then I believe that. They had great examples from their parents, and I just want to make sure you're all right with this huge commitment. But above all, I'm just happy for you and Lucia. You deserve happiness after what you've been through."

"Thanks, Loretta. I love you and we'll talk soon. I'm pulling into work now so I've gotta go."

She blew me a few kisses before we hung up. Our conversation had made me even more certain about what I was doing than I had already was. Hearing my own thoughts out loud just confirmed it: I was sure about this and about him.

When I got home from work, I was exhausted. It was one of those days when a lot of my employees had issues. In helping them, I didn't have time to attend to my regular duties. However, putting out fires often came with the job, and we had to adjust to it. When I got home later than usual, the house was quiet, so I thought

Dominic and Lucia were in the other room, perhaps putting away her ballet stuff. I placed my stuff down on the breakfast bar and walked straight to the sofa to meld into it.

Just as I was starting to doze off, I heard Lucia speaking to me, and I snapped out of my daze to find her walking toward me.

"Momma." I patted the sofa so she could sit next to me.

"Yes, baby." I watched her face contort with sadness.

"I'm scared, and I need to ask you something." I could tell she was on the verge of tears.

"Baby, you know you can ask me anything. Please tell me so I can fix it."

She climbed into my lap and clung to me. What kind of help could a six-year-old need?

"Lucia, tell me what's wrong. You're scaring me now. You can tell me anything, you know that, don't you?"

Her eyes looked like spring water pools on the sidewalk, filling with tears that leaked down her face. I hugged her to me fiercely.

"There's a daddy-and-daughter dance in the spring. My teacher told us when she sent home the calendar the other day," Lucia whispered into my chest. I pulled her back to look at her again. Her eyes bore into mine, begging me to understand, but what she was talking about didn't register until she blurted out, "But I don't have a daddy."

I choked. My chest tightened as if it were filled with concrete blocks. And there it was: the time when she needed a daddy and didn't have one. Lucia had not asked any more questions after we'd seen Alex in the park that day, but now with this new development, it made her not having a father even more obvious. I also knew that she loved Dominic as much as he loved her and that a part of her just wanted the security of knowing where she stood with him. I understood that feeling—that need—more than anything.

"Oh God, baby. I'm so sorry." I held her to me and rocked us back and forth.

She began speaking in a slow and unsure manner then finished with a rush of words. "Momma, umm ... c-can I ask, um, Dominic if he'll be my daddy?"

I almost laughed, my stupid nervous laugh, because she sounded so cute and vulnerable. And I'd be damned if I had an answer for her. In all honesty, I had no idea what to say in that situation, so we sat there crying until I felt the sofa sink down and Dominic's arms wrap around us. He must have been coming from his room and heard us talking from the hallway.

Dominic reached for Lucia and led her to his lap. He held her face in his hands and wiped her tears away. "Sweet, sweet girl. If that's what you want and if your mom is okay with it, then I would love nothing more than to be your dad. I have been thinking about that for as long as I've known you. I love you, sweet girl. You're an amazing, loving, talented, beautiful, precious, and sweet little girl."

Hugging her to him, he swayed back and forth while he said those beautiful words. "Any daddy would be proud to have you." Dominic pulled back and kissed her nose, right on the tip. And *I* was suddenly a blubbering mess.

Lucia, on the other hand, was beaming. She jumped up on his lap, wrapped her little arms around his neck, and squeezed with all her might. And as he wrapped his arms around her, too, I could see his face turning red from her tight grip. It was sweet, honest, and just what they needed.

"Yes, please. Be my daddy."

I mouthed thank you to him, and he just nodded. His beautiful green eyes shimmered with tears like droplets on a wet spring leaf, and I knew in that moment that without a doubt he did want to be with us forever.

Chapter 20
Marbles

This year for Thanksgiving, I had invited all of my relatives, as I had done every year. Dominic had also invited his, but none of them could make it. Instead, it was just going to be my Los Angeles clan: my dad, Susan, and maybe Danielle, her husband, and son if they didn't have plans already.

Cooking big meals for holidays always gave me joy. Italians' need to express love through food was supposedly ingrained; this rang true for me because, along with the desire to have a huge family, I always wanted to bring everyone together with big meals. I'd learned how to cook the typical Italian foods from my aunts and uncles growing up. They'd also taught me to have food in the fridge at all times just in case someone stopped by. The first thing one of them would do when anyone would visit was to heat up food the old-fashioned way on the stove and plop it down in front of their guest, whether or not he had asked for it. My mother had never cooked big meals since it was just the two of us and it was much more difficult to cook for two than ten. So, now that it was my turn to cook the big meals, it made me feel like I had my own big family. Everyone was so busy all the time, nowadays they only seemed to get together on holidays.

❧❧❧❧

Soon enough, it was time for Lucia's first ballet dance recital. She was quite nervous because she was afraid of letting us down. Dominic and I had reassured her many times that she couldn't do anything that would disappoint us. I was in crazy mother mode and called all of our friends to invite them. Lucia may have grown up without a father, but she wasn't lacking in love or loved ones. Susan and my dad were coming with us, and I had invited Danielle and her family. What surprised me was that Danielle's son, Gabe, was excited to go. In all honesty, I had expected him to skip out on watching a bunch of little girls dance, but he really wanted to support Lucia.

So, with my camera charged, we went to the Kirk Douglas Theatre in downtown Culver City. The newly-refurbished, rectangular building had a long marquee and a tower on the side that was all lit up with bright lights. Culver City used to be a big part of the filming industry, and this building was part of that history. For this recital, the dance company had gone all out. They laid out a red carpet for the performers and had photographers taking candid shots when the dancers walked in. Inside, a corner was set up with a single, professional photographer and a few different backdrops. The dance teachers posed with their classes as groups, and each child got a professional picture of him- or herself. All of the kids were beaming from ear to ear while they strutted around like little movie stars.

Susan and I went to our seats, as instructed by Mrs. Caprisi, while she took the dancers backstage. Dominic and my father stayed in the lobby to wait for Danielle, Gary, and Gabe. There were plenty of places to sit because everyone was still loitering in the lobby, so I nabbed seven seats in the first row. I was nervous for Lucia, and Susan tried to distract me by filling me in about her and Vitto. He had accepted the incredible job opportunity that was offered to him, and he had moved here a few weeks ago. He was busy moving and settling into his new home and said it was taking time to adjust to his new job. It was wonderful knowing he was so close, even though I hadn't seen much of him since he'd gotten here because he had been spending all of his free time with Susan.

The lights started flashing, and I felt Dominic touch my shoulder so everyone could squeeze by and take their seats. Dominic sat next to me and wrapped his arm around my shoulders. Then he leaned in and whispered, "I can't wait to see her dance. She's been practicing so much and is so intent on making you proud."

The warmth of his breath so close to my ear sent chills down my spine, and I shivered. God, this man could excite me anywhere, but I needed to concentrate on what he'd said. "She thinks I'm not proud of her?" I whispered with a frown. That was upsetting.

"Calm down, she just wants to do well for you, that's all. Don't get all worked up."

I looked at him straight on and searched his eyes to try and interpret his mood. He didn't seem angry, but his tone did.

I let out a long breath. "I'm not getting worked up. I'm fine. Why are you so . . . so snappy?"

"I just want you to enjoy the show and not sit here and stew."

I understood he didn't want me to ruin the night by worrying, but he didn't have to scold me. Maybe it was because he'd spent so much time helping her prepare for this night that he felt just as much responsibility for wanting us to have a good time.

❧ ❧ ❧ ❧

The performances started with the smaller children first. Little three- to five-year-olds were on stage with their adorable costumes, trying to remember their moves. One girl kept going off and doing her own thing, and she had the whole audience cracking up. We watched all of the different age groups do their dances, and I thought they all did very well. My nerves were just starting to get the best of me when Lucia's group came out on stage and danced to "Boyfriend" by Justin

Beiber. I thought they were a bit young to be dancing to that song, but they were amazing. They were more refined, and it looked as if they hit every beat and actually stayed in sync throughout the number. The seven of us hooted and hollered when they finished, and my hands burned from clapping so hard.

Tears began to fall down my face, and my heart constricted a little. My baby was growing up and accomplishing things on her own. Although I was proud of her, it hurt to know she would need me less and less as she got older. Dominic must have seen my face or sensed my mood, because he pulled me closer to him. He peppered my temple and hair with kisses, whispering sweet words to me. When the whole production was over, the head of the dance academy called out each group for their applause and standing ovation. All the men with us had brought flowers for Lucia, so when it was her turn to step forward and bow with her group, they all ran up and presented the flowers to her. The girls ran off stage with grand smiles and full arms.

Filing out of the theatre, we waited for Lucia in the lobby. We were taking her for dinner at our favorite restaurant, Paco's. When she saw us, she came running into my arms.

"Did you like it, Momma?"

I squeezed her to me and held on tight. "I loved it, baby. You did so well— fantastic! I think your group was the best of them all," I told her with pride.

She beamed from the praise and ran off to hug all of her guests, thanking the men for her flowers.

ৡৢৡৢ৶ঌ৶ঌ

We had a wonderful evening with our family and friends, but I couldn't wait to get into bed with Dominic that night. When I crawled into his arms, we kissed and touched. His soft fingers were roughening up a bit, and they felt so good running from my ankle to my knee and up to the apex of my thigh. He made sensual circuits like that, alternating from leg to leg.

"Stop teasing me," I said while trying to pull him up toward my face. He wouldn't budge and chuckled at me.

Dominic covered my abdomen and hip bones with kisses before he licked from one all the way to the other. Then he blew on the whole area, sending goose bumps over my body. I crossed my legs at my feet and began rubbing them together, trying to distract myself. Dominic flattened his large palm and dragged it up my body, touching every bit of skin he could along the way until he reached my neck. His hand went behind my head, and he lifted it so he could crash his mouth to mine. When we connected, I felt a spark flash go through me. My skin lit up in flames, as it did every time we melded. Moving slowly and savoring every moment, we allowed our bodies to speak. He kissed my lips raw with passion, and when our eyes connected, we fell apart.

We had gotten pretty good at the whole lovemaking thing. Our first time had been intimidating for me, but now I felt like we'd found our rhythm. Some nights, we'd take it slow and let our emotions control us. Others, our animalistic side would come out, and we'd tear and claw at each other. But the best nights were when we'd laugh and talk and have fun. I'd crack a joke, and he'd pretend he was upset at me for "ruining the moment." At first, he was surprised that I could actually laugh and speak while he was seducing me, but something would set me off—it may have been the way he kissed my skin or tickled me when he touched me—and once I'd get going, there was no returning. I'd have the giggles so bad I couldn't stop. The first time this happened, Dominic didn't want to continue until I had stopped laughing, but I couldn't. I'd been mad at him for leaving me hot and bothered, but then I rolled him over and rode him, all the while teasing him until we were both laughing. Together we discovered that sex had many facets and all of them were just as important, and this knowledge and experience brought us closer together. We learned so much about each other. I knew every inch of his skin, where his moles were, and where he was ticklish. He learned I liked to bite when I became overzealous and almost took off his nipple.

We also had our most personal conversations in the dark after we'd make love and were feeling vulnerable. Dominic worried I would hold back because I was afraid of getting hurt, and I worried the same about him. One night, I asked him if he missed his old life: the fast pace, his family, his ex-fiancée, or anything from before us.

"No," he said. "I don't miss any of it. Well, I miss my parents a bit, but not in the way you may think. We would have dinner, all of us, on Saturday nights, but otherwise we didn't see each other much. We were all too busy. I don't miss the hustle and bustle of the city or that fast-paced life at all. *This* right *here* is where I want to be. I want what I have now, you and Lucia. I want ballet practice and recitals and trick-or-treating and movie nights and holding you in my arms every night. And I know I want more with you two as well — more of this."

Dominic took a deep breath and continued. "You know, I believe in fate, the ultimate plan that is designed for all of us. So, I believe that I had to follow every path I've been on to get to you. If I had found you years ago, maybe I wouldn't have appreciated you the way I do now. And I think the same goes for you. Your life's path led you to me, and we were always meant to be together. It's our destiny."

He spoke with such conviction that I knew he meant every word of it. And the more I thought about it, the more I believed he was right. We were meant for each other.

Chapter 21
Knucklebones

As much as I hated it, the thrill of shopping for our Thanksgiving meal was vibrating through me. Pushing my big metal cart through the grocery store and focusing on what I needed kept me from freaking out about the crowd. This was the best time to shop because stores had everything one would need to cook Thanksgiving dinner in the middle aisles. The procrastinator in me waited until the day before the holiday, so I was happy for the ease of it.

While I was loading the grocery bags into the car, my cell phone rang. I popped the Bose earbud hanging around my neck into my ear, and pushed the button on the mic, and answered without even looking to see who was calling.

"Hello," I said, out of breath from lifting all the bags.

"Yo, cuz, what's up?" Vitto asked.

I laughed. "Nothing. Whatcha doing?"

"Chillin'. But, seriously, I wanted to know if you needed help cooking?" Vitto was an excellent cook. He had learned from his father, who had taught me also.

"Um, how's this? Come over anytime you want tomorrow, and whatever needs to be done at that point, you can help with. Sound good?" I didn't want to bother anyone with helping me. Plus, cooking was cathartic, and I enjoyed it.

"Sounds good. Susan and I will be there early, so what can we bring?"

"I guess you can bring some beer. Whatever kind you like. Okay?"

જીજીરીરી

On Thanksgiving Day, we had a full table, and my resulting smile was huge. Dominic sat at the head of the table, with Lucia and me sitting on either side of him. My dad sat at the other end of the table, Susan was next to me, and Vitto was next to Lucia. We were all holding hands, heads bowed, getting ready to say grace. Lucia cleared her throat, and Dominic told us that she would be saying the prayer.

When he announced that, I lifted my head so I could spy on the two of them. Lucia squirmed in her seat for a moment but settled down soon after.

"Well, I want to thank God for the food, my mom for cooking, and our family for coming to spend this day with us. I want to thank God for my momma and my dad."

A few gasps were heard around the table.

"I thank God for sending him to us and for him loving us. Thank you, God. Amen," she finished, her voice strong and confident.

"Amen," we all said in chorus.

Susan was sitting next to me, and I gave her hand and Dominic's a tight squeeze when I said my "amen." I looked up at Lucia and reached both of my hands across the table to her. She placed her hands in mine, and I squeezed them, too. "I love you. That was a great prayer," I told her with all the love in my heart. Then I snuck a look at Dominic, and he was beaming. He looked so happy to be here with us. His eyes sparkled with pride when he told Lucia how great her prayer had been.

We stuffed ourselves silly, and the turkey made us all very tired. After dinner, we lounged around having a few drinks and talking. It was nice to catch up with everyone.

I decided it was time to get the dessert ready and brew a pot of coffee. While I was in the kitchen getting things together, my dad strolled to the counter. I looked over my shoulder while I pulled the apple pie from the oven.

"How are you doing, Dad?"

"I'm doing good." Then, "I wanted to ask you something," he whispered so no one else would hear him.

I turned around in a flash to look at his face. It was impossible to gauge his expression, because it was blank. I couldn't read him at all. He was much better at hiding his feelings than I was.

"What? What is it, Dad?" I asked, concerned.

"Well, I'm not trying to interfere, but I want to know what's going on with Lucia calling Dominic 'dad'." My father's voice was steady and bold.

I was taken quite aback by his tone, so I flinched a little, and he saw it.

"I'm not sure what you mean," I said more to steady myself.

"Mia, you haven't known this guy long, and you're already letting her call him 'dad'?" he asked as if I were doing something wrong.

How dare he?

Fire ramped through my body, and I took immediate offense at his words. I was raging mad. "I do know him and my judgment should be enough, but you don't believe I'm capable of making good decisions, do you?" I asked while shooting death rays from my eyes.

"Well, it seems as if you've had a huge lapse of judgment. You throw out Alex and jump right in with Dominic. I mean, don't you think this is too soon?"

"No, Dad, I don't think it's too soon. There's not a timeline for these things. And I did not throw away anything with Alex. He is already remarried and having—or has already had—another child. So, if anyone moved on a bit too quickly, it was him. But who am I to judge? The bottom line is, he didn't want Lucia. Dominic does! He wants me and her, and he loves us just as much as we love him." I looked my father straight in the eyes to show him how serious I was, refusing to back down to anyone who wanted to stand in our way.

I knew everyone in the house could hear us. Dominic stood up and walked over to my dad.

"Paul, would you step outside with me for a quick word?" Dominic asked. I knew he'd set my dad straight, but I was still fuming; we shouldn't have to explain ourselves to anyone.

Turning back to the stove to act like I was finishing with dessert, I tried to get myself together. I needed to let the anger roll off of me and calm down. Someone come up behind me, but I stayed busy at the stove, not turning around to see who it was.

"Hey, Mia. Don't be too hard on Uncle Paul. Dominic is wicked cool, and Uncle Paul just needs to get to know him better. They haven't spent much time together, have they? He just wants to make sure you and Lucia don't get hurt again, you know?" Vitto placed his hand on my arm, and his presence calmed me. I turned to him, and he pulled me into his arms. "It'll be all right."

I nodded into his chest. "You're right, I just don't want anything ruining what we have. Sometimes I'm just waiting for the other shoe to drop instead of being able to enjoy this happiness." I looked up at him. "Thanks, Vitto. I'm so glad you're here. Now we just need Lori to move here, too, and we'll be all set!"

"Are the pies ready? I'm dying for some pumpkin pie." Always the hungry one, Vitto stayed to help me while I glanced over my shoulder to spy on Dominic and my dad on the balcony. They were leaning on the railing with their backs to us in what looked like a deep discussion.

Vitto helped me serve the dessert and coffee.

Before he left, my father apologized to me for butting into my business. I answered him with a grunt, dismissing him. My feelings were hurt, and I still needed time to cool off.

◈◈◈◈

Our nightly ritual of movie watching was exchanged for something different. After the conversation with my father, I needed the connection with Dominic.

The minute Lucia was asleep and we went to our room, I pushed Dominic against the wall and began ripping his clothes off. He looked like he'd been through a tornado by the time his Queen t-shirt was off. My lips were on his, rough and needy, pushing my tongue into his mouth. Ever the attentive one, he turned us, and then pushed me face first into the wall. My breathing was coming fast, and my lungs were heavy. He stripped off my clothes, popped my bra like a professional, and grabbed my panties from the side and pulled. I moaned.

He kicked my legs apart and took me right there, hard and fast. My left cheek was pressed against the wall, and his hands were over mine, splayed out on the wall. It felt like he was touching every inch of my body at once, and the slick sweat served as the glue that stuck us together. We didn't speak—no words were needed—but the sounds of our rough lovemaking filled the room. My hair was wet and sticking to my face, my back, and Dominic. I recognized the taste of salt from his sweat when it dripped into my mouth.

Falling over the edge with such pleasure had washed away all of my anger and frustration.

Dominic's mouth went to my ear with his final spasm. "Ahh, I love you," he whispered.

"Love you, too." I felt as if I was splattered against the wall; not a muscle in me was able to move. "Shower?" I croaked out.

He tried to keep his lips attached to mine while he picked me up bridal style and carried me to the bathroom.

Dominic kicked the lid to the toilet down and sat me on it before starting the shower. I leaned my head to the side against the wall and closed my eyes, feeling like rubber and completely drained. When the water was warm enough, Dominic reached a hand out for me. Once the water hit my skin, I began to revive. I turned to face Dominic with body wash in my hands and caressed his torso while I washed him. Running my fingers over every inch of him, I reconnected with him in a different way—a more sensitive way. We were making love with our souls and our minds instead of with our bodies. I looked up to see his face and caught him staring down at me. Immersed in our moment, in our deep connection, I told him with my eyes how much I loved and appreciated him.

৵৵৵৵

Later, I wanted to ask Dominic what he said to my father and where they stood now, but I didn't want to ruin the moment.

"What is it?"

I smirked because Dominic was very good at reading my face.

"What did my dad say to you?"

Dominic looked away for a moment. I knew by his expression he didn't want to talk about it. He didn't want to cause friction between my father and me. I understood, because I didn't want any problems with him either, but I needed to know.

"He was just concerned about you and Lucia. Look, he didn't want Lucia to get attached, call me 'dad,' and then have things not work out between us. He needed to know how serious I am about this relationship with not only you, but with her as well. It's a big deal, and I understand his concern."

"Whatever it is, you can tell me," I coaxed.

"Okay, here it goes," he mumbled. I kept my eyes glued to his, searching to try and catch a glimpse of regret or distress.

"You know that I love you and Lucia so much and that I want to be a part of this family very much, right?" Dominic's eyes bore into mine, waiting for an answer.

I didn't need to think about it; the reply flew from my mouth as soon as he'd finished speaking. "Of course I do."

"Well, your dad brought up a great point, and it's one I've thought about myself, so don't get any angrier with him, okay?"

I nodded, waiting for him to continue.

We lay together in the bed. He pulled me to him and held me close while he spoke into my hair. I could feel his warm breath fan out on the side of my face and forehead. It was soothing.

"So, if I'm going to be a true part of this family, I can't stay home all day and not contribute financially. I need to get a job and make money and help in every way I can. And I've thought about this, tried to plan it out in my head."

He paused to see if I had anything to say about it. In all honesty, I wanted to hear his plan before I freaked out.

"I have skills in accounting and can work from home and, when I get some clients, I can spend a few hours at their office consulting, teaching, and picking up paperwork. That way I can still be here when you and Lucia need me, but I will be bringing in some income. I have a small trust fund that I started using after I lost my job, but it won't last forever." He took a deep breath and let it out between scattering quick kisses on my head. "I just need to contribute monetarily, too, you know?"

Because I was torn, I wasn't sure what to say. Somehow, I managed to gather my thoughts and speak my peace.

"I understand that there is stigma attached to a man who doesn't bring home the bacon, but I don't agree with that. I've saved over the years and, even though I don't make tons of money, I do make a good living. The condo is paid off, and Lucia has a college fund, so if we budget, you wouldn't have to work." Then I sighed because I hadn't phrased that right. "I'm sorry. What I was trying to say is: I'm not with you and I don't love you for what you can provide us, but I understand that as an equal partner in this relationship it's important for you to contribute fully. And I think your idea is great, but only if you can tell me you'd be happy doing it."

I felt him relax. "Thank you," he said. "And yes, I'd be very happy because I could do it on my own time, and it's not in some fast-paced world that's going to tie me down. This would be my own business. When Gary and I were talking about my old job, he told me he knew a bunch of small businesses that need an accountant. The job could pay well, and I could make my own hours." Dominic's shoulders twitched in a small shrug.

"I'll support you in whatever you want to do, and I have all the faith in the world in you," I said truthfully.

He bent down, kissed my lips, and adjusted the blankets around me before settling down for sleep.

Chapter 22
Pick-up Sticks

Dominic told me his parents were coming for Christmas since they hadn't been able to make it for Thanksgiving. I was anxious but excited to meet them. He described how his mother was sweet and his father was funny. Even with his constant words of encouragement, I was still nervous.

The closer to Christmas we got, the more anxious I felt. I wracked my brain over what to get Dominic for a gift. The man owned everything he wanted and could buy anything he lacked, so I needed to get him something we could enjoy together. He tended to be a very generous person, so I was hoping he wouldn't splurge on me. I mean, I had no problems accepting gifts—I welcomed and loved them—but I didn't want Dominic to go overboard. His unconditional love was the best gift he could ever give me. I was sure he would love the meaning behind my gift to him, since it would lead to us being naked on a private beach somewhere.

Lucia had been acting in a suspicious manner lately, as if she were hiding something. I found it strange; she was in a constant state of giggles and always snickering behind her hand. She had Dominic wrapped around her finger and was spending a lot of time with him— more than usual, and without including me. I asked and asked what was going on with the two of them, but they both said it was nothing.

My nerves were already strung like an archery bow, since I was hosting both Christmas Eve and Christmas dinner for guests I had never met. Even though I had always wanted to, I had never cooked for so many people. It was exciting because most of my relatives were going to be there, but stressful because I wanted it all to be perfect. Lori and Chris were coming, and Susan and Vitto had agreed to join us as well.

୨·୨·ଏ·ଏ

It was the morning before Christmas Eve, and I was getting ready for work. Lucia had started school vacation already and was enjoying the time off. Dominic had been busy helping me around the house and visiting with his parents. They had arrived a few days prior, and every evening they went out and did some sightseeing. I was happy Dominic was able to spend that time with them.

His parents were wonderful, so down to earth and not at all what I had expected. The things I'd heard about Dominic from Lori and from the stories he told me about his childhood made me picture them as uptight, high society types. The truth was, they were so sweet that I felt comfortable with them immediately.

We met the night they arrived, and we went out to dinner at a great little Italian place, San Genaros, in downtown Culver City.

Dominic wanted Lucia and me to join them for more sightseeing, but I was just too busy with work and preparing for our holiday feasts. He asked if he could take Lucia with him and his parents, which warmed my heart, and without a second thought, I agreed. Every night, Lucia came back with more giggles and whispers, but with the biggest smile on her face. I knew that her relationship with Dominic was just what she needed—what they both needed.

One morning on my way out the door to work, I found myself trapped in the hallway when I heard Dominic and his mother speaking in the kitchen.

"Are you serious? You're one hundred percent sure about your decision?" asked Emma. I held my breath, not knowing for sure what they were discussing, but I had an inkling it might be about me. I leaned against the wall next to the doorway so they wouldn't see me.

There was a heavy sigh and the silence of a long pause before Dominic began to speak. "Mother, I've never been so sure about anything in my life," he said with conviction.

"It's just that you were engaged not too long ago to Porsha, and I thought you were sure about that. She didn't come with the same kind of baggage," Emma said. Her words didn't sound mean, exactly; she just sounded like a worried mother. Either way, I still felt a pain in my heart.

"Mother, please stop it. First of all, Lucia is not baggage. Never—" His voice cut off, and then I heard him sigh again. "Look, I don't know how to make you understand this. From the moment I met Mia, I knew I'd love her. It wasn't like the love I thought I felt for Porsha. It wasn't arranged or expected; it was my heart's choosing. I need those girls, and they love me, too. I mean they *love* me, by choice — not for anything I have to offer them. I know that I will have a life full of love and happiness with them. I'm not looking through rose-colored glasses, either. I know with any relationship that's worth having, there will be hard times, but I also know that what we have will get us through any struggle that may come. The relationship we have now is still new, but it's already so much more than I ever had or felt for Porsha. Mia and I allowed our relationship to take its course; we didn't try to stop it or rush it. It happened as it should have, and I will be forever grateful for having met her," he said with so much strength in his voice that it made me fall in love with him even more.

"Oh, honey. As your mother, I'll always worry about you and your brother. I just need to make sure you both are happy. And I see that you are, and there's nothing in this world that makes me happier than that." Her voice cracked. It sounded like she was crying.

"Thanks, Mom. I want you to get to know them and see how wonderful they are." Dominic's voice was muffled.

I cleared my throat and walked toward the kitchen, acting surprised that Emma was there.

"Good morning, Emma. I didn't know you were here." They were standing next to a bar stool, hugging, but they broke apart at the sound of my voice. Dominic looked at me with concern while his hand scrubbed furiously at the scruff on his chin.

"Good morning," I said to him, and I rubbed his back when I walked into the kitchen.

"Oh, good morning, dear. Do you have to work today? We sure would like you to join us sightseeing," Emma said.

"I'm sorry. I do have to work, but we have all weekend to do things together." I looked around. "Where's Dom Sr.?" I asked.

A worried look crossed Emma's face. She covered it in a flash, but I saw it. "He's resting at the hotel today. Said he was too tired and thought that it was jet lag."

I looked at Dominic, and his brows scrunched together. So, his mother's comment hadn't missed his notice, either.

"What a shame. I hope he feels better. Let's hope some rest will do it." Then I looked toward Dominic and said, "I'll be home for dinner, and maybe I can cook this time." I laughed because I doubted Dominic would let me.

From his reply, he thought it was funny as well. "Yeah, I don't think so, honey," he said and pecked my lips.

"Lucia's still sleeping?" I asked, though I knew she was or she would have been out here with us. I was stalling, not wanting to leave.

"Yes, she is. I'm taking them to the Queen Mary cruise ship today. I'm excited to see it for myself."

"Well, you three have fun, and I'll see you later. Call me if you need anything, okay?" We kissed and I squeezed him in a hug, wishing I could go with him instead of heading off to work.

 প্র প্র ওণ ওণ

Dominic was our savior and our reward for what we had gone through. Lucia and I had survived so much heartache, disappointment, and failure that Dominic had to be our light at the end of the tunnel. Still, there were things I had to work on personally, and I knew that. I understood the amount of effort involved in being in a relationship and keeping it—and my heart—safe. One of the first things I'd learned from my experience with Alex was that, if you didn't continue to work on keeping your love alive, you could forget about keeping it at all. I knew I was happy with Dominic, and he made Lucia happy as well. He was invested in our lives. He treated Lucia as her own person. His affection for her was not conditioned on our feelings for him; it just existed on its own. Their developing relationship was so beautiful to watch, and it made my heart swelled with happiness.

Dominic was a gentleman with impeccable manners, and he had a sort of old-fashioned way of thinking about relationships. I was learning to be okay with it, respecting his ideas on working and wanting to take care of us, even though I knew I could handle it on my own. It was all about give and take, and if that was important to him, I could give it to him.

I was also under no illusion that our lives would be perfect. We hadn't lived together for very long, but one day, we'd feel more comfortable with each other and have a real fight or I'd snap at him for no reason. He'd get to know me better, too, and get sick of my bullshit at some point. I didn't want to fight, but I knew that was part of a true relationship and was looking forward to getting there.

Those were the thoughts that ran through my mind whenever I remembered the things my father had said during Thanksgiving. Yes, I had been insulted at his lack of trust in my judgment, but now I wondered if there had been a little truth in what he'd said. Nothing in life was guaranteed, but I knew I would give my all to this relationship because I had never felt for Alex the way I felt now for Dominic. I also knew that Alex had never loved me the way Dominic did. Our lives were fated, and what happened between us was the way it was meant to be. I wasn't going to play hard to get or fight what we deserved.

ᔿᔿᕉᕉ

A few days before Christmas, with the little time I had left, I wrapped all of the last-minute gifts and put them under the tree. Our house looked so amazing. It wasn't overdone or gaudy; it was perfection. I had always wanted a white tree, so Dominic had gotten us one, and we bought red lights and bulbs to decorate it. While shopping throughout the year, I had found different types of snowflake ornaments and bought each one I saw. We also had ten big silver rings the size of a grapefruit with a twirling snowflake in the middle. I found five big, white, sparkly snowflakes with a small red bead in the center, as well. A bunch of small ornaments just like the big ones were hung onto the three garlands I'd strung around the banister on the balcony. The garlands had small, white lights with cranberries that we all strung ourselves. We had tons of candles and other lit decorations placed in a strategic manner all around the house.

I loved Christmas, and I knew this was going to be the best one ever. Lucia and I had more loved ones to spend it with this year, and that was the most special part about it.

Chapter 23
Tag, You're It.

I woke before the sun rose, feeling excited and nervous. The room was dark, and Dominic was still sleeping. There was so much to do to prepare for our first Christmas Eve and Christmas Day celebration. I wanted it to be perfect. Tiptoeing out of the room, I went to the kitchen where I brewed myself a cup of coffee. Trying not to make too much noise, I began to prepare all the dishes for the traditional Christmas Eve Feast of the Seven Fishes.

The tradition called for us to make seven fish dishes to represent the seven sacraments. I had marinated and salted everything two days prior, and all the vegetables had been prepared the day before. Today, I had to pull it all together. I started with the *cioppino*, a delicious soup with vegetables and four different types of seafood. The second dish was a baked, stuffed fish served with rice pilaf. The third dish was a sea bass with an herb butter and frisée salad — and the list went on. Homemade cannoli would finish off the big meal.

Immersed in my work, I felt Dominic wrap his arms around my waist. "Mmm, you smell so good. Or is it the food?" he joked with his nose buried in my neck.

I reached behind me to smack his shoulder, laughing. "Both, baby."

He squeezed tighter and left a trail of wet kisses down my neck. It felt so good, but I had so much to do.

"Where do you need me to start?"

I looked around and contemplated his question.

"Oh, I know. Can you get the china down? And the silver? You can just put it on the table for now. I have to wash it all."

"You've got it, babe. I'll even wash and dry them for ya."

I looked at him, and he had the most beautiful smile plastered on his face. "You're in a great mood today. Any particular reason?"

He shrugged and shook his head. His beaming smile subtly changed to a smirk.

Before I could read into that, Lucia came barreling out of her room. "Momma, Daddy, everyone's coming today, right?"

"Yes, my little munchkin. I'm going to need your help later. We have a very special night ahead of us," said Dominic. Watching their interaction, I tried to figure out what they were up to.

After breakfast, Lucia began decorating the table. She made little stockings out of construction paper and put our names on them. Then she cut tons of different sized snowflakes and scattered them around the table on top of the red tablecloth. I told Dominic where I had stored some Christmas candles for the table, and he got those down as well. The house was beginning to look like a true winter wonderland.

For Christmas Day, I had all of the traditional foods fixed, and Susan was in charge of the turkey. Once I had everything pretty much done, I ran to shower because I knew our guests would start to trickle in soon to snack and lounge. This arrangement was fine with me. Since I'd moved to California, I had missed being around people I loved, cooking together, and making new memories. This year was special; I had most of my family with me. One person was missing: my mom.

While I was in the shower, Dominic called in to say he was getting Lucia ready and that they would pick up his parents at their hotel. The timing was perfect, since it allowed me to get ready in peace.

After my relaxing shower, I went through my beauty routine, applying lotion, deodorant, perfume, and face creams. I put some frizz serum and mousse in my hair and let it air dry. Next, I put on a calf-length black skirt, a silver shimmery sweater, black tights, and black knee-length boots. It was formfitting but, to my surprise, comfortable. *And sexy*, I admitted as I twisted and turned to check myself out in the mirror.

Just as I was slipping on my jewelry, I heard the front door open. *Perfect timing.*

I walked out of our bedroom to see Dominic and his parents standing in the living room. I started to greet them when I noticed an unexpected person in the room. I jumped in place, but then ran over to hug her fiercely.

"Ma! Oh, my God! What are you doing here? How'd you get here?" I was crying, so excited to see her.

She just laughed and squeezed me tighter, whispering in my ear, "Your handsome man arranged the whole thing."

I was soaking my mom's shoulder in my tears, and I was ecstatic to have her with me. I didn't think she would care—I didn't!

Letting her go, I turned around to find Dominic sitting with his parents and Lucia on the sofa. I ran to him and, he stood up to catch me. I jumped into his arms and hugged him hard.

"Thank you so much. Thank you." I heard everyone giggle at my exuberance. Turning around, I faced Dominic's parents. "I'm so sorry for being rude." I hugged his mother first. "Emma, thanks for being here." Then I turned to his father and hugged him, too. "I'm so glad you are all here."

"Mia, you know there's no other place we'd rather be than celebrating the holidays with all of you."

I smiled wide at Emma's sincerity. "Aw, thanks! You guys have no idea what this means to me. I haven't had a big family dinner since I was in high school."

We sat on the sofa catching up while Dominic got everyone a drink. I mouthed a thank you, and he blew me a kiss in return. Lucia sat on my mother's lap the whole time, absorbing all her love while she could.

"So, Mia," Emma said, "Dominic tells me you made a whole Italian spread for tonight."

Her face lit up while I explained the meaning of the Feast of the Seven Fishes. "But tomorrow we're doing the traditional Christmas dinner," I said.

At that, her whole face glowed, and her smile rivaled the lights on my tree.

"Oh, yes, tomorrow." She grabbed my hand and, with a firm grip, wrapped it in hers. "I'm just so happy to be here."

I watched Emma loosen up and touch me more often with small hugs and gentle arm squeezes. She even began complimenting me. This treatment was quite different to how she had been when we'd first met. Not to say she was ever rude; just very polite and reserved.

"Momma, when is everyone else getting here?" Lucia interrupted us.

I looked at her, still sitting with my mother. "Soon, baby, soon. You want something to eat?"

"Yeah, I'm hungry." I stood up and excused myself, asking if anyone else wanted anything. My mother followed me into the kitchen.

"Mia, I'm so happy for you. Dominic seems wonderful," whispered my mother.

I smiled at her over my shoulder while I made Lucia a sandwich.

"He is, Ma. I can't believe he pulled this off without me knowing." I shook my head. What a sneaky, wonderful man.

"I know. He called me weeks ago and asked me to keep it a secret. He's been planning for a while," she answered.

"I wonder if that's what he and Lucia have been so secretive about," I said.

A mischievous smile spread across her face, but she just shrugged.

🙟 🙟 🙜 🙜

The next time the doorbell rang, Lucia jumped for joy. Warmth from the cooking was filling the condo and the joy from our arriving family filled my heart.

"Hey, cuz! Merry Christmas!" said Vitto with a big hug. Susan walked in right behind him.

"Merry Christmas, Vitto" I said, and then turned to Susan with open arms. "Merry Christmas, girl. You look happy."

She laughed while we hugged. "I am. He's amazing. I just can't believe I didn't meet him sooner," Susan said.

"Loretta! Oh, I've missed you," my mother screamed when Lori and Chris walked in. My mother grabbed Lori in a tight embrace.

The before-dinner entertainment was watching my mother and father make small talk. They always did such a good job of being cordial and never saying anything bad about each other. I appreciated it a lot.

The girls helped me set out the stuffed mushrooms I had made, along with a bowl of olives, a plate of cheese and crackers, and a few bowls of mixed nuts. We snacked for a bit while we all sat around and caught up. The condo was full, but I wouldn't have had it any other way.

Chapter 24
K-I-S-S-I-N-G

I stood up from the table and raised my wine glass.

"I want to thank everyone for coming tonight. It has always been a dream of mine to have my own big, family dinners, and your presence has given me that. This is a beautiful Christmas! Thank you, everyone." Truthfully, I wasn't able get out everything I felt inside because I was so overwhelmed with happiness.

"Cheers!"

We drained our glasses. As I sat down and looked at the faces of everyone I cared about, new and old, I couldn't help but think about how Lucia and I had survived great pain and how much our luck had changed. In the end, she had a full family, and I knew they would all be steady people in our lives.

Dominic's face was shining like Polaris. He was the most beautiful sight I'd ever seen. We stuffed our faces, and I was very pleased when I received plenty of praise from Emma and Dom Senior. After dinner, we had coffee and light desserts, and we spent the rest of the evening talking, singing Christmas carols, and playing games to keep Lucia busy.

Just as I was about to put Lucia to bed, Dominic asked if he could give me one gift before she had to go. I was flummoxed because Santa had to come soon and I didn't want her awake, but I agreed. Dominic's silly, puppy dog expression was impossible to deny. It was pitiful.

Once I said yes, everyone around us scrambled into place while Dominic pulled me to the tree. Confused though I was, I had a feeling that the others were in on this moment somehow. I looked around, trying to read the expressions on everyone's faces, but they all looked the same. The women had their hands clasped to their chests with bright smiles, and the men were wearing cocky smirks. *Strange!* Dominic and I stood in front of the tree with our audience beside us, apparently waiting for something with bated breath.

"What's everyone looking at?" I whispered to Dominic.

He chuckled. "Us, baby."

Oh, like *that* was a great explanation.

He reached down under the tree and seemed to struggle with something. When he won the battle and stood back up, I gasped.

"Oh, my God! What are you doing?"

In his hand sat a beautiful ring, which was poking out of a black satin box. When I looked up from the box, Dominic went down on one knee. His beautiful green eyes were shimmering like fresh raindrops on a blade of grass.

"Mia, I never knew what love was until I met you. I had almost lost hope that I would be a father or a husband one day. You and Lucia have given me more than I ever dreamed of or deserved. You love me unconditionally, and I promise to do the same. I also promise that you and our children will always be my first priority. I love you with all of my heart and soul. Mia, will you marry me?"

I was sobbing, and I couldn't stop. Through my ecstatic tears, I replied enthusiastically, "Yes, yes I'll marry you! I promise you all of those things and more!"

I pulled him up and hugged him with all of my might. He pulled back, and, in what seemed like slow motion, placed the ring on my finger. Savoring every moment, I gazed at his beaming smile, and I vowed to always make him look that way. I was so consumed by the moment that I almost didn't hear everyone cheering and yelling out their congratulations.

Dominic kissed me on the lips, and then I held my hand up in front of me to see how the ring looked on my finger. Nestled in a bed of platinum sat a beautiful, princess-cut diamond. It was *perfect!*

I looked around at our closest family and friends and saw their eyes shining with tears of joy to match our own. They rushed over and surrounded us in warm hugs. Emma and Dom welcomed me to the family, and I saw the sincerity in their faces. I looked over and caught my dad giving Dominic one of those half man-hugs. All the emotions running through me were almost too much.

Then Dominic cleared his throat. He had Lucia in his arms.

"I have a few more things I want to say. Part of my proposal is for Lucia as well. Lucia, will you officially adopt me as your father?"

She laughed. "You supposed to adopt me," she said to Dominic before looking at me for confirmation. "Right, Momma?"

"Yes, baby, you're right, but he wants to make sure you want him, as well."

She nodded with excitement. "Yes! We adopt each other." That settled it, and I thought it was the sweetest thing I'd ever seen.

Susan and Lori gushed over my ring, telling me how happy they were for me.

Dominic interrupted all of the excited voices. "I have one more thing to say—or ask, rather." He looked quite nervous. "I want to marry you as soon as possible and to take advantage of having both of our families here. So, with the help of the people that mean the most to us, I've arranged for us to have a ceremony tomorrow. In the morning." The last words he dragged out, and I could see the uncertainty in his face. Dominic didn't want to upset me; he wanted to make this a memorable time.

He continued, "We'll have to do this at the courthouse when it opens to make it official. There was no way I could have gotten a marriage certificate without you finding out my plans. Okay?"

I wasn't upset, just very shocked. "You did what?" Surprised by the secret itself, I figured out what everyone else had been up to. All the strange looks and secrets between Lucia and Dominic made sense now. "Did you know?" I asked Lucia.

"Yes, I helped pick your ring and decorate for the wedding," she squealed.

"How did you do it, Lucia?" I looked at her in shock. At her age, she shouldn't have been able to keep a secret so well.

"It was the most important secret ever," she said with such conviction that I laughed.

I glanced at Dominic. He was waiting for my answer.

"So, are you okay with getting married tomorrow? I didn't want a courthouse or a Vegas wedding. I wanted a nice ceremony with our friends and loved ones."

"I'm very okay with this. I'm just overwhelmed. I can't believe you would go through all this trouble for me." This was a gift, and I was ecstatic that he'd thought enough about our wedding to plan it for us both. I looked at everyone in the room: my mom and dad, Dominic's parents, my cousins, and my best friend. They all had a part in this, and it was for me. "Thank you, everyone. You have no idea what this all means to me."

"So tell me, what's the itinerary?" I continued.

The women swept me to my room, and after I put Lucia to bed, we sat around going over a few details of my wedding. They gave up the time schedule and said the rest would be a surprise. Everyone stayed that night on blow-up mattresses and spare beds. We had a long and special day ahead of us, and no one wanted to miss a second of it.

Susan dragged me out of bed by seven in the morning and pushed me into the shower. I was scheduled to meet Dominic at the altar at ten in the morning, and Lori informed me that the men had left already. They had to finish setting up and would get ready at the venue.

I drank some coffee and ate a light breakfast while the girls did my hair and makeup. Lucia came in wearing a silky, bright red dress with a white sash around the waist and white tights and shoes. She looked beautiful. Her hair was half up and secured with a white ribbon, while the rest of her curls cascaded down her back. She carried a white basket full of red rose petals in her small hands.

"I'm the flower girl, Momma." Her proud smile was infectious.

"You lucky girl. That's an important job."

"Nana and Grandma got me ready."

"Well, you look beautiful, baby girl. I love that dress!" She twirled around in circles so the skirt rippled in the air.

Time passed in a flash, and soon, the girls informed me it was time to leave.

"Mia, Lori and I wanted to tell you how happy we are for you. You found a wonderful man who was made just for you and Lucia. We're so happy to be here with you." My tough-on-the-outside friend, Susan, began to cry, and it touched me so much that the dam just broke. Lori joined in and hugged us with love.

"Everything in life happens for a reason. If it weren't for Lori, I would never have met Dominic. If I hadn't been with Alex, I wouldn't have had Lucia. Without

Lucia, I wouldn't have had a reason to meet Dominic. I'm just so happy, and that word doesn't even seem big enough to describe what I feel." I giggled, the happiest I had ever been in my whole life.

We stood to slip on my dress. Lori pulled open the dress bag and, with caring concentration, slid out the most beautiful dress I had ever seen. It had spaghetti straps and a sweetheart bodice. Lace and satin shot out from the waist in a long skirt, which had a train several feet long. My favorite part was the big, red satin sash around the waist, matching the color of Lucia's dress. They had chosen my favorite color as the accent, and I loved it. Everything was perfect.

I stepped into the dress with care, not wanting to ruin it, and I looked in the mirror, feeling beautiful. My hair was styled like Lucia's, but instead of a ribbon, I had a dainty, diamond-like tiara placed on the top of my head. My make up was light, natural, and just right for me. The dress fit just right; I wondered how they knew my measurements.

"Girl, we've been dressing you for years," Susan responded when I asked. "I'm glad it fits so well."

"Thank you! Both of you! I'll never be able to repay you for all you've done for me."

They waved me off like I was crazy, but they had both been by my side during my most difficult years.

"Let's get me married." I grinned and turned around, calling, "Mom, Emma, we're ready."

I walked out into the living room and saw both mothers standing in similarly beautiful dresses. Each dress was a different shade of cream: Emma's with a small jacket, and my mother's with cap sleeves. They were both knee length and form fitting, as both women had great figures for their age.

Lori and Susan came out wearing red dresses that fell a few inches above the knee and had the same sweetheart neckline as my dress had. They were simple but very elegant, and the color also matched Lucia's dress.

"So which one of you wants to be my maid of honor?"

Lori laughed and looked at Susan. "We already decided that I'd be the maid of honor and Susan would be the bridesmaid."

I smiled and shook my head. "God, could you make it any easier to get married? I haven't had to do anything."

My mother and Emma each wove an arm in mine, and we walked to the elevator together. When they chose the button for the lobby instead of the garage, I knew we'd be walking to our destination.

My mother was the first to crack. With a knowing smirk, she revealed, "We're going to the clubhouse."

The clubhouse sat on the lake, surrounded by trees; it was a beautiful setting for a wedding. I wondered how they'd set it all up. It had the potential to be the ideal spot to get married.

We walked along the concrete path to the clubhouse until I could see the outside of the building. A big, wooden deck hung over the lake, decorated with white tulle, two big Christmas trees framed a staged altar, and red and white lights draped everywhere. The day was overcast, so the lights stood out in the haze like beacons on a boat.

Emma and my mom walked me around to a door that led us to a small room by the kitchen area. They practically shoved me into the room; I supposed it was so Dominic wouldn't see me.

"By the way, who's marrying us?"

Susan piped up. "The husband of one of my co-workers is a Justice of the Peace, and he agreed to do this for us." Wow, they'd thought of everything and put so much time and energy into this. I was so grateful for all they had done—and now, I was ready to get married.

Chapter 25
Pitching Pennies

There was a knock on the door, and my mother opened it to reveal my father looking dapper in his tuxedo. My father was a handsome man, and I'd been told that I looked just like a female version of him.

"You ready, sweet girl?" He came over to me with a box. "This is for you from your mother and me. We pitched in to get 'your something new'." He opened it, and inside was a beautiful set of earrings. They were made up of three diamond bubbles, one that sat on the ear and two more that dangled beneath the first. There was a matching necklace with the same three bubble diamonds; all three were simple and elegant—just my style.

I hugged my dad and mom forcefully. Just then, Emma came forward with two small boxes.

"Dom and I have fallen in love with you and Lucia. You both make our son very happy, and we are so grateful to you for that."

"You don't have to thank me for that, Emma. He's very easy to love and makes us just as happy as I hope we make him," I said, smiling at her.

"Thank you, dear. Well, we wanted you both to have something from our side of the family." She turned to Lucia and continued. "For you, Lucia. These were mine. Dom bought these for me when we first started dating, years and years ago." Emma opened one of the boxes and pulled out small diamond studs. She asked Lucia if she could put them in her ears, and of course, Lucia responded with a resounding 'yes.'

"Wow, thank you, Grandma. They're beautiful," said Lucia. I was trying hard not to cry.

Emma stood back up and faced me again. "Mia, this is for you. This was my mother's, and she gave it to Dominic to pass on to his wife on his wedding day. So, for today it's 'borrowed,' but after the wedding, it's yours." She pulled out a beautiful white gold tennis bracelet that nearly matched the jewelry my parents had given me.

"Thank you so much, Emma. These are so precious, and we'll cherish them always." I hugged her again.

Lori and Susan came forward with my "something blue." They handed me a blue garter, which Susan reclaimed and slid up to my thigh in two seconds flat. So far, the day had been filled with many thank yous, happy tears, and hugs.

My dad cleared his throat and said, "Well, it's time to get the show on the road."

He led me out through the party area of the clubhouse and through the back doors to the deck. The decorations were clearly planned and thoughtfully placed in a theme that matched our Christmas decorations. Lori handed me a beautiful bouquet of red tulips and gerbera daisies, my favorite flowers.

I made my way straight to Dominic. Standing in between the two Christmas trees against the railing of the deck, he was a sight. The lake and trees were a striking landscape for this occasion. The wedding song, Pachelbel's *Canon in D Major*, played from the speakers that were placed around the balcony, and Dominic's eyes pulled me to him. His smile was genuine and bright, and, like the lights all around him, it lit up the cloudy sky. He was dressed in the most flattering tuxedo a man could wear, and he looked like a million dollars. Every inch of him was pristine. Everything else disappeared. I didn't watch Lucia walk down the aisle and throw her petals, or Susan and Lori lead the way before me—they were just distractions. My eyes were focused on my other half, standing there watching me with reverence and ready to make me his. I was so blessed to have found him.

After what seemed like an eternity, I arrived at Dominic's side. I just wanted to touch him and strengthen our connection.

My father shook Dominic's hand and said, "Take care of my baby girl."

"Forever, sir," answered Dominic.

With those words, my father placed my hand in Dominic's and went to his seat.

My handsome fiancé mouthed, "Beautiful," and I whispered back, "I love you."

The Justice of the Peace began the ceremony, and I was a little confused. However, it didn't matter, because my body was calm while I stood gazing into Dominic's eyes. His positive outlook on life had been such a life-changer for me. Soaking up his love and losing myself in his closeness, I thought about how lucky I was. I listened to his words of love and commitment and waited for my turn to speak.

We swore to love and honor each other, and all I could think of was the kiss at the end of it all. A magnetic force was pulling us together, filling me with the need to touch him and be close to him. Those feelings were overwhelming, and I thought he shared them because his beautiful apple green eyes bore into mine.

The current that flowed between us when he placed the ring on my finger made my breath hitch. Once I'd placed the band on his finger, I looked up to see his jaw tense in pleasure. I understood the pure satisfaction in seeing our rings on each other.

"I now pronounce you husband and wife. You may kiss the bride," said the Justice of the Peace.

Instead of leaning in to kiss me, he winked at me mischievously. Then, he called Lucia forward from her place behind me. Bending down, he looked her in the eyes and said, "Lucia, I love you so much and am so blessed to have you as my first child."

He pulled a small box from his pocket and opened it. Inside was a dainty white gold ring that wrapped around to form a heart on the top. The ring had a small diamond attached to the dip in the heart. It was simple but lovely, and perfect for Lucia's little finger.

"I promise to love you, care for you, protect you, and guide you for all of your years. I promise to be the best father I can be, and you will always be my baby girl." Dominic slid the ring on her right forefinger.

Tears of happiness fell from my eyes, and when I looked up, I saw everyone else was tearful while they watched this tender scene play out.

Lucia hugged Dominic and said, "Thank you, Daddy. I promise to love you always, too!"

Dominic scooped Lucia into his arms, and not a moment too soon, he and I kissed to seal our marriage and our family's union. In a playful moment, we both smooched Lucia's cheeks while she soaked up the attention.

Everyone began blowing bubbles in our direction, which excited Lucia enough to jump down from Dominic's arms so that she could seek out some of her own. Before we could go back to the condo for Christmas dinner, all of our guests made Dominic and me pose for pictures with everyone in every imaginable combination. It had been the most amazing day of my life, and we still had so much left of it.

෨෨෨෨

Our group made such a ruckus on the way back to the condo that several people came out of their town homes to see what was happening. Many of them gave us their congratulations, and others clapped for us. It felt like I was using Cloud Nine as my transportation home.

No sooner had we opened the front door than I smelled the turkey. One of our guests had thoughtfully started to cook it before we left for the clubhouse. My smile widened—everyone had done so much to make this day perfect.

Before I could change, my mother wanted pictures in front of the Christmas tree, so Dominic and I obliged her. Not a moment too soon, I was in our room preparing to slip off my gown. Dominic entered just in time to assist me with the zipper. Of course, he couldn't just leave it at that. With great care, he slid the small straps down my shoulders. Then he held onto the bodice while he worked the dress down my body, allowing me to step out of it.

"I'll get it. You get dressed," Dominic said. I watched for a moment while he hung up my dress, and then began to undress himself. I wanted to do that for him, but I knew that, if I tried, our family would be eating Christmas dinner without us. Snapping out of my daze before he could catch me, I stepped into the closet behind him and pulled out one of my most comfortable pairs of black jeans, a cute t-shirt that Lori had given me that said "bride" on it, and a pair of ballet flats.

I couldn't help myself; when I saw Dominic bend over to pull up his pants, I ran my hand from the back of his thigh, over his ass, to his lower back. *God, he has such a nice butt!*

He turned around to face me, laughing. "Babe, you know I want nothing more than to ravish you right now, but our house is full of our family, and the food needs to be prepared."

"You're right, but you're just too fine for your own good," I said.

Hurrying to put on our clothes, we raced each other out to the living room like little kids. I beat him by a foot, but only because I was smaller and could squeeze around him. Turning to Dominic, I gave him a pat on his rump and said, "Let's get to work."

The kitchen wasn't big enough for all of us, but we made do by having some people work in the bar area while Dominic and I moved in and out of the kitchen. He did wonders with the table again, placing fresh linens and clean silverware at each setting. We had some different decorations, like snowmen and shiny stars, to set around the table and pretty name cards that Lucia had made because she wanted assigned seating.

The room was buzzing with small conversations, and everyone was very involved in their own tasks; the entire scene warmed my heart. Dominic and I kept sneaking glances at each other, and then we would smile, finding it difficult to believe we were really married. It all seemed so surreal and dream-like, but I knew in my heart this day and this marriage were perfect for us. It had been the right decision, and that's why it hadn't been difficult for me to agree with everything he had set up. Perhaps to some people it would seem like we had moved too fast and gotten married too soon, but I knew deep down in my soul that this was it. He was my one and only true love—my soul mate.

୨ଓ ୨ଓ ଓ୧ ଓ୧

Two hours later, after my father's toast, all that could be heard was the sound of forks clanking on plates. There was very little chatter. Everyone was stuffing their faces as if they hadn't eaten in days.

"So, where you guys going on a honeymoon?" Vitto asked.

Dominic shook his head. "I didn't have time to set anything up, and with Lucia in school, I figured we would have to wait until the summer."

My eyes lit up, and I thought about my Christmas gift to Dominic: a huge coincidence that would turn out well for both of us.

"You know, we haven't opened our Christmas gifts yet. After dinner, we'll get on that," I said with a big smile on my face, proud of my purchase.

Lucia began shoving food in her mouth after my announcement.

"Slow down, Lucia. You still have to wait until everyone's finished," I said with a laugh.

Dominic leaned over and whispered in my ear. "I hope you're not upset that I didn't organize a honeymoon."

I turned to look him in the eyes, and his fear of letting me down reflected in them, so I reached for his hand and squeezed it.

"You have nothing to worry about, Dominic. I still can't believe you were able to pull off a wedding on your own and without me knowing. So, no, I'm not upset at all. In fact, I'm quite happy you didn't take care of the honeymoon, too," I said.

He didn't know what to make of my comment; I could see by the confused expression on his face.

Chapter 26
Tic-Tac-Toe

We decided we would open gifts during dessert and coffee while we sat around the tree. Dominic was in charge of passing out everyone's gifts. Poor Lucia hadn't even gotten to open any of the gifts Santa had left for her, so she tore into those first. Then, Dominic brought in the new bike that had been hiding on the balcony, and she screeched so loud, I almost lost my hearing. Dominic looked like he'd won the lottery while he watched Lucia's excitement. My heart could not expand any further or it might burst out of my chest; experiencing Dominic's first Christmas with a child in the house was a treat I'd never forget.

When the gifts were all opened and the guys had picked up all the trash, I decided that the time had come to give Dominic his big present.

Reaching into the tree, I pulled out an envelope and hid it behind my back.

"Dominic, there's one more for you," I said, and everyone stopped what they were doing. Dominic's eyebrows rose in surprise, and my excitement grew.

"I thought I'd opened everything."

"Nope. Open this," I said and handed him the envelope.

Reading the printed itinerary, Dominic shook with laughter. He looked up at me with such amusement that all I could do was laugh, too. The appropriateness of my gift was the icing on our already-perfect cake.

Dominic's face suddenly changed, and he squinted at me. "Did you know?"

I was still laughing. "No! I swear," I said, shaking my head.

"Well, what is it?" yelled my mom.

Dominic looked up with a handsome smile on his face. "Two open tickets to Hawaii," he said.

Laughter erupted from everyone in the room. *Classic.*

"Yo, cuz', that's wicked awesome! I swear you two are perfect for each other!" yelled Vitto.

Over the next week, most of us had to go back to work, but we did have New Year's to look forward to. Our visitors were still going to be in town, and all of us planned to celebrate together. Dominic suggested we rent out our wedding venue, the clubhouse by the lake, to ring in the new year. The idea started off simple but grew into a big party with caterers, a DJ, and a bunch of our friends.

Vitto and Susan had become a lot more serious in a short amount of time, and I found it endearing. Since I loved being in love, I wanted everyone around me to be in love, too, and it seemed like most of my friends were. It warmed my heart that Vitto had fallen into step so quickly in L.A. I had been afraid that he wouldn't last three months away from our family back in Boston. At times, I thought Susan had a lot to do with his smooth transition.

I had begged and begged Loretta to move here, but she said that until she'd made it big, New York was her home. I understood her reasoning, and I was happy for her because she had a dream and was pursuing it. Chris, a sweetheart just like his brother, confessed that he'd go wherever Lori went. He could find banking work anywhere.

Having everyone living near us became my next goal. I explained to Emma my desire and wondered if she would consider it. She looked shocked that I'd asked her, but I was sincere and honest with my request. To her credit, she promised to consider it, since being close to Dominic was as important to her as being close to Chris. She felt torn between her boys, which was understandable.

Dominic spent the week before New Year's with Lucia, his parents, my mom, and Chris and Lori. I spent the weekdays working and the nights with my family planning for our party.

One night in bed after we had made love, Dominic pinned me with a question that I had been too busy to think about up until that point.

Wrapped in his arms with my head on his chest, I listened to his heart thump against my ear. He squeezed me a bit tighter, and so I craned my head to look at him. From his expression, I knew he wanted to talk about something serious.

"What is it, Dominic?" I asked, concerned.

"I've been thinking, and I just wanted to ask. No pressure, okay?"

"Okay," I said.

"Well, I want to know how long you would like to wait to have more children."

Thinking about his question, I skimmed my fingers up and down his thin line of hair from his chest to his stomach. "Would I sound too anxious if I said now? I mean, I just didn't think I would have an opportunity to have more kids. So, yeah, I'd like to get on it, pronto."

He leaned down and kissed me hard on the mouth. Pulling back, he looked at me with excitement. "Just what I wanted to hear," he said.

∽✐∽✐✐✐

A few days later while I sat at my desk working on timecards, my desk phone rang.

"Good morning. This is Mia. May I help you?" I asked.

"Mia," said a voice I hadn't heard in a long time. "It's Alex. Do you have a minute?"

113

"Oh. Uh, what's up?" I stuttered, the surprise evident in my voice.

"I'll make this brief. My mother has been bugging me since the divorce to see Lucia. She's bitched me out over my decision and can't believe I'd give up her granddaughter," he said.

Secretly, I agreed with her, but it was too late. "So, what does she want exactly?" I asked with trepidation.

"Well, she wants contact with her, and when she comes to visit me, she'd like to see her, I guess," he explained.

I sighed heavily, not even trying to hide it. "Listen, she has a father now. I'm not sure about all this. I mean, I don't want to confuse her. I just . . . I don't know. I'll have to talk to her father," I said, emphasizing the word "father" every chance I could.

"Yeah, okay. I see. Well, will you call me and let me know?"

I agreed to call him and asked for his number. Then, I dialed Dominic in a panic.

"Hey, baby. How's your day going?" he asked.

"Dominic, Alex called and said his mother wants contact with Lucia," I said. Dread had entered my body the second I had heard Alex's voice, and his request made me extremely anxious. I knew at this point I sounded hysterical to Dominic.

"Babe, listen to me. Just calm down. There's one thing you have to remember: he gave up rights to her. He is *nothing* to her. Get it?" Dominic said, and I made a non-committal noise in response. "So, that means it's up to us, and that's all. We'll talk about it when you get home, but you shouldn't worry."

"Okay, yeah. That makes sense. You're right. Okay, I just need to calm down," I answered.

"You all right now?" he asked.

"Yeah, much better. What are you guys doing today?" I asked to change the subject.

"I'm going to take them to Hollywood to see the Chinese Theatre and walk around the mall over there. They don't want to do too much; they're a little worn out," he said.

"I bet they are. You have been going non-stop." I sighed, feeling better already. "All right. I've got to get back to work. We'll talk tonight."

"Yes, baby, we'll talk tonight. I love you."

A smile was brought to my face. "I love you, too. And, Dominic . . ."

"Yeah?" he asked.

"Thank you."

❧ ❧ ❧ ❧

Winter in Los Angeles was cold for us locals, but according to people like my mother and Dominic's parents, it was a reprieve from their typical, bitter winter. I had become so accustomed to California temperatures that I froze at night when the sun went down and the breeze from the ocean cooled the air. During the day, it was warm enough for a light jacket or sweatshirt and our East Coast guests loved it.

My nerves were calm by the time I got home for dinner, and that surprised me. Looking around the house, I noticed it looked empty. I wondered where everyone was so I called out, "Dominic?"

"In here," he said, his voice coming from the direction of our bedroom.

Throwing my purse and keys on the bar, I ran toward my solace. I found him sprinkling rose petals on the floor around the bed. The glow from candlelight cast shadows on the walls, and the dozens of roses placed on every surface looked almost black in the darkness. The curtains were closed to block out the light of the moon. Our room had been transformed into a romantic love nest. Looking at Dominic, I saw the blush filling his cheeks.

"Hey," I whispered. I was shocked that he had gone through all this trouble for me, and I had no idea why.

"Hey," he replied.

"What is all of this?"

When he stretched his arms out to me, I walked right into them. He embraced me tightly, showing me that I could count on him always to comfort me when my thoughts and fears got the best of me.

"It's for you — for us." He kissed the top of my head. "Everyone is gone for the night. My parents have Lucia, and your mom is staying the night with Vitto. But before we start the night, we need to talk. Let's go out to the living room." He pulled back and gestured toward the door.

"Give me a minute? I'd like to change first," I said.

I quickly changed into a sweat suit and my fuzzy Ugg slippers and met Dominic on the sofa. Sitting sideways with my back against the armrest, I laid my legs over his. We were closer this way, and my position allowed me to see his face.

Dominic rubbed soothing circuits from my thighs down to my feet. "So, tell me about Alex's call," he said, his voice steady and calm.

I took a deep, cleansing breath and gathered my thoughts; I had been considering it all day.

"Well, I'm torn. I mean, I've known his mother my whole life, and I hate to feel like I'm being cruel. But I think the logical thing to do is go with my gut, and my gut says they really have no right to request anything from us. I don't want to confuse Lucia more than she may be already. She doesn't even know his parents because she's only seen them a handful of times, and that was when she was a baby. So no, I don't think I want to disrupt our family at all. Alex should have thought about all of this before he just walked away without a second glance in my daughter's direction. And I'm not being spiteful," I continued.

"Good. I agree because I want to do what's best for Lucia. I'm not concerned with anyone else's feelings." Dominic kissed my forehead. "So, do you feel okay about telling him no? I mean, since we agree?"

I caressed his cheek while gazing into his beautiful, caring eyes. "I do, and thank you for being here for me — for us." I leaned in and touched my lips to his. "I love you," I mumbled against his mouth, and then kissed him with all my love.

Dominic placed one arm under my legs and the other around my waist and stood. He walked us to our room so we could enjoy the romantic atmosphere he had set up for us.

We spent the next few hours expressing our love for one another.

Chapter 27
Stone Skipping

Seven glorious months later, Dominic and I found ourselves in Hawaii for our long overdue honeymoon. It felt so strange to be away without Lucia, but time alone couldn't have been more welcome. Vitto and Susan had begged to take her to New York for part of their vacation so she could visit Dominic's parents, Lori, and Chris. We thought it was a perfect idea. Lucia's excitement over flying for the first time was palpable, and Dominic and I were sorry we'd miss it. We all promised to talk on the phone or Skype daily so Lucia wouldn't get too homesick.

I'd booked us at the Moana Surfrider Resort in Waikiki. The pictures on the website did not do it justice. The grand hotel stood like a palatial plantation home right on the beach. A row of rocking chairs followed the front lanai. The entry into the foyer was lined with columns all the way to the front desk. Candle lanterns hung from the ceiling of the lobby, and the whole setting brought tears to my eyes. I had never seen a plantation-style home in person, and somehow I felt so welcome in that hotel. Beyond the definition of beauty, the hotel also had a lot of history. In 1901, it became the first large hotel in Waikiki, and soon after, became a hangout for the Olympic gold medalist in swimming, Duke Kahanamoku. Restored to its original look, the hotel was an amazing sight.

"Baby, look at this amazing hotel. God, I'd love a house in this style," I said.

"It is really nice, honey, but I don't think California has too many houses in plantation style."

"I know," I groaned.

After we checked in, we found ourselves in the tower suite, where we got ready to hit the beach. Our room was lavish with a bed that was bigger than king size. Stepping down from the bedroom area, there was a living room with sofas, a table, and chairs. Looking out the sliding glass doors, I saw a big lanai with two lounge chairs for sunning. The view of the blond sand and the vast blue ocean stretched out before us. Tall, thin palm trees swayed in the light ocean breeze, and the scent of flowers blew back at us.

Dominic stood behind me with his arms wrapped around my waist while we gazed out at the beautiful view.

"I'm so happy to be here with you," I said, looking up at him.

He smiled down at me with his gorgeous mouth and sparkling green eyes. "There's no one else in this world I'd rather be with than you, so wherever you go, I'll always follow." He bent down and kissed me.

We spent a few more moments appreciating the view, and then Dominic decided he wanted to shower so we could go out and explore the beach. While he was in the bathroom, I leaned against the railing of the balcony and thought about what had happened in the past seven months since our wedding.

Both of our families had worked hard to stay close, even though many of us lived far from each other. I spoke with Lori and Chris most often, and they had even come to visit a couple of times on long weekends. My relationship with Dominic's parents had grown, as well. I spoke with them a few times a week and had come to care for Emma so much. The love she had for her boys made me respect her even more. She wanted them to be happy, and it showed in everything she did. Thinking back even further, I knew that when I had overheard her conversation with Dominic in our living room, it was her way of ensuring he knew what he was doing. Emma wanted to know he was thinking not only with his heart but also with his head. She looked out for her boy, and when he'd confessed his love for Lucia and me, she knew he meant it and had thought it out. From that moment on, she had been on board.

Vitto and Susan had become a very serious couple. My crazy, fun-loving, silly cousin had finally settled down. He'd found a woman who could handle his loud, boisterous, Italian mouth, and one who loved him despite all his immature flaws. He had grown so much with her. Vitto had always been a very intelligent man, but he was not always sensible; Susan had helped him be both. When he asked her to move in with him, she made him move in with her instead. He didn't care; he just wanted to be with her. I had a feeling that, before the year was over, he'd ask her to marry him.

Dominic, as promised, started his own accounting business with the intention of keeping it low key. Starting with just a few select clients, his skills became known to a few bigger businesses that soon fought for his services. He tried in vain to keep it small, but he ended up with more than a handful of customers. The bigger companies had employees inputting all of the expenses into a bookkeeping program, while Dominic just reconciled everything and checked over their calculations. His work was not overly time-consuming—he still spent plenty of time with Lucia and me—and they paid well for his services. The smaller companies paid Dominic to do everything they needed, and he was able to accomplish it all from our dining room table. The amazing part was, he managed to work while Lucia was in school and still had dinner on the table most nights by the time I got home. With Lucia on summer vacation, he'd work a few hours every day and set Lucia up next to him with her own busy work. She'd read a book or work on some workbooks he'd bought to prepare her for her next year of school. He truly was the best man I had ever known. No one could ever understand my gratefulness for meeting him and the hoops he went through to keep us happy.

When Alex had called and begged us to allow his mother to see Lucia, it was a difficult time for me. I didn't want to seem like an unreasonable person, but my feelings weren't important. All that mattered was what was best for Lucia, and allowing her to become acquainted with people who didn't know her was not a good decision. A short time after that, the paperwork we'd filed for Lucia's legal adoption was finalized. Dominic made another adoption certificate on the computer for Lucia because she'd adopted him, too, and they both hung up their certificates with pride. My heart swelled at the thought of them choosing each other—something so much more special than loving someone just because you were supposed to.

We had also been trying in vain to make a baby, but much to our disappointment, nothing had happened yet. At first we made love to show how much we felt about each other, but then when I wasn't getting pregnant, we began making love just to try and conceive. It still hadn't worked. My heart ached at the thought of not being able to give Dominic this one thing he wanted so much. If my period was late for even a day, my hopes would soar, only to be crushed again, month after month. I had heard from many people that when you actually *tried* to make a baby it was almost impossible, but when you just let go it would happen. So, without giving it too much thought, we hoped this vacation would relax me enough to let go.

"Babe," whispered Dominic from behind me. I jumped a mile. I'd been so caught up in my thoughts that I hadn't heard him come up behind me. He laughed at my startled expression. "You okay, there?" he asked.

"Yeah, sorry. Just thinking," I answered.

He kissed the side of face and pulled me into a hug. His clean scent filled my nose and warmed my heart.

"I love you," I mumbled into his chest.

"I love you, too, babe. Why don't you go and get ready so we can enjoy the sun on the beach, okay?"

I nodded, and with a gentle shove from Dominic, I was on my way.

જીજીજીજી

Before jumping in the shower, I tied up my hair. It felt good to rinse away the recycled air from the airplane. I always felt so gross after flying. Since I knew that dirty airplane air was in my hair as well, I decided wash it after the beach. Cleaning it too many times in one day would damage it. I threw on a cute bikini, a pair of shorts, a tank top, and my favorite pair of flip-flops. Then, to avoid sun damage, I put some moisturizer and a strong sunscreen on my face.

"Dominic, I'm ready," I yelled when I walked out of the bathroom. I found him on the lanai, sitting on one of the lounge chairs.

With a few towels and a bag packed with sunscreen and books, we headed down to the beach behind the hotel. People were spread out all over the sand, some under umbrellas or soaking up the sun's rays, and others doing all sorts of water activities. The sand was hot under my feet, and the sun wrapped me in a warm cocoon. We opted for a spot with an umbrella for a small fee. To the left, Diamond Head volcano sat, protruding out into the ocean, and to the right, the beach stretched on for miles. Once we were lying down on the lounge chairs, Dominic reached for my hand. We read while holding hands, stopping every once in a while to comment on something. It was easy to distinguish the professional surfers from the newbies receiving lessons. Surfing looked like a lot of fun, perhaps something for us to try together. We discussed things we'd want to do during the coming two weeks. I wanted to climb Diamond Head, and Dominic wanted to get Matsumoto's famous shaved ice in the North Shore. The hotel put on a huge luau every night with dinner service, which we were excited to attend, and I also wanted us to do couples massages. Of course, some days we didn't have to plan anything.

A few hours of sun did us good, but soon we were starving. Dominic suggested we go back up to shower and get ready for a nice dinner somewhere. Walking through the lobby, he stopped to speak with the concierge, who suggested a restaurant with French cuisine, Michel's, a short drive away. We rushed upstairs and pulled out our dressy clothes. I wore a linen blue dress, and Dominic wore a Hawaiian shirt with embroidered hibiscus flowers in the same shade of blue.

The restaurant was beautiful, set right on the beach near Diamond Head. They had outdoor seating surrounded by billowing palm trees and a perfect view of the sunset. The sky turned different shades of purple, orange, and pink that reflected on the ocean. The lights from the restaurant lit the greenery that framed the balcony, and shadows played on the sand that looked as dark as dirt. We were engulfed in the most romantic setting. Sitting at a small table for two next to the railing, we had the ideal view of it all.

The menu, which was full of decadent choices, made my mouth water. The decision to choose between *cioppino* and blackened ahi seemed too difficult to make, but eventually I decided on the former. Dominic ordered the New York steak with a bottle of white wine. We held hands over the table, made goo-goo eyes at each other, and whispered sweet nothings all throughout dinner. I was sure we looked either adorable or sickeningly sweet to onlookers; I loved every minute of it.

Dinner tasted sublime, and we decided to drive back to the hotel and walk around for a while. Dominic held me close while we kicked off our shoes and walked along the beach. The sand had cooled off, and the beach was lit by tiki lights.

"You know it's almost been a year since you came to us?" I asked.

"Yup," he answered.

"This has been the best year of my life, and I'm sure Lucia would say the same thing." I said.

Dominic stopped walking and pulled me to him. He wrapped me in a tight embrace and kissed the top of my head. Just being surrounded in the essence of his love sent chills up my spine.

"Mia, this has been the best year of my life, too. And I know every year I get to spend with you will get better and better. You have given me so much, and I'll never be able to thank you for it all," he said while he gazed into my eyes, lighting me up like a firecracker.

"You don't ever need to thank me for loving you." I licked my lips and felt my heart pounding in my chest. "I want to go to the room now, please," I begged.

He broke away from me and began running. "I'll race you there," he said into the wind.

I laughed and took off after him like my life depended on it.

Chapter 28
I Spy

The first morning, I awoke to Dominic's hands and mouth turning my world upside down. My body stiffened, my toes curled, and my back arched when it shot over the edge. I was panting deeply, and my skin was moist with a sheen of sweat.

I grabbed Dominic's shoulders, trying to pull him up and over me.

"Come here, baby," I panted.

He slinked his way up, kissing every inch of my torso, my neck, my face, and finally my mouth. Dominic's lips covered mine in a hungry kiss. His whiskers made the kiss feel rough, but it was offset by the warmth of his mouth. With one hand, he held himself over me while the other still caressed and explored my body.

"Hmmm." The sound vibrated from Dominic's mouth, and I moaned when our tongues tasted one another. *What a way to wake up!*

The sound of waves crashing and birds chirping barely entered my awareness. The sun was already shining high in the sky, lighting the room brightly.

With Dominic settled between my legs, we connected in every way. The sense of going home always washed over me when we joined together like that. I lifted my feet to his ass and pushed him closer to me, wanting more.

"Stop it. I want to go slow and make love to you," he said into my neck.

"I don't want slow. I want it rough and fast," I demanded.

"Later. I want to love you like this first. Now, shush. I'm busy," he grunted.

Not able to deny him anything, I melted into his soft caresses and slow movements. I ran my hands up and down his back, scraping my fingers down his skin in pleasure. God, I loved his body, his skin, his face — everything about him. I wanted to be devoured—*consumed*—by him. Being that close felt right, as if we were magnets with pulls so strong that we couldn't be pulled apart if we tried. This man owned me, body and soul. Soon, my body tensed, and stars shot out from behind my eyelids. I held on to his biceps so tightly that I left bruises. Dominic trailed little kisses with slight bites down my jaw and neck while he groaned in pleasure. My moans became more and more high pitched until I just let it all go and crashed in a wet spot on the bed.

"Wow, thanks for the wakeup call," I said with a chuckle.

His body rested over mine, and his weight held me in place. My arms tightened around him, not wanting to let him move.

"Mmm, so good," he said.

"Love you so, so much," I whispered in his ear.

He lifted his head, bit my ear lobe, and said, "I love you, too."

We opted to shower together because we didn't want to separate, not even for a moment. Imitating his slow, worshipful mood, I took my time and washed him with soft, caring hands. In turn, he did the same for me. Our shower took about an hour too long, but it was necessary to stay in the tight bubble we'd created.

I was ready to try some of the infamous Hawaiian coffee. We went down to The Veranda restaurant for a delicious breakfast and the best coffee I had ever tasted.

"You know, we need to call Lucia after breakfast. I miss my little munchkin." I looked up at Dominic with wide eyes. "I just realized I've never been away from her since she was born. It feels great though. Should I be guilty?" I asked with a nervous chuckle.

Reaching across for my hand, Dominic soothed me. "No, babe. You shouldn't feel guilty at all. You have always been there for her, and if she needed you right now, you'd be there. You need time away, as well. We need time together as a couple sometimes. You're a wonderful mother," he said.

I nodded, because he was right. I had and would always be whatever Lucia needed, but there were times when I needed to be myself, not just Lucia's mother.

"Are we going to the North Shore today?" I asked.

"If you want, or we can go to Diamond Head."

"Let's hurry so we can call Lucia; then we'll decide," I said.

$$\wp\!\wp\!\wp\!\wp\!\wp$$

Back in the room, I dialed Susan's number.

"Hello?" she answered.

"Hey, how are you?" I asked.

"I'm great. How's Hawaii?"

"It's wonderful — beautiful, actually. Um, is Lucia around?"

She laughed. "You're so transparent. Yes, she's here."

I sighed in relief, dying to hear my daughter's voice.

"Momma?"

"Hey, baby. How are you? I miss you so much," I said.

"I miss you, too. Where's Daddy? Are you guys having fun?"

She was so cute, and it made me feel good that she was excited to speak to us as well.

"Yes, we're having fun. And Daddy's right here. You want to talk to him?"

Dominic was all smiles when I handed him the phone.

"Hey, baby girl. Yes. I know, I miss you, too. Yes, we did. Okay, I'll tell her, and we'll call you tomorrow, okay? I love you, too."

I leaned into the phone and yelled, "Love you." I heard her happy screeches through the receiver before she hung up.

Dominic was silent for a few moments, rubbing his hand along his jaw. His eyes were unfocused, and I could see the wheels turning in his head.

"I was thinking — how about we fly straight to New York from here? We can catch a flight from LAX to JFK and meet Lucia there. We could spend a week or so sightseeing together," he suggested.

"I need to see if I can get another week off. I have enough time saved, but I only asked for these two. Let me email my boss and see what I can do," I suggested.

ভ৹ ভ৹ ৶ও ৶ও

Since we had gotten off to a slow start that morning, Dominic and I decided that we'd go hiking on Diamond Head volcano. A drive to the North Shore was about an hour, and we wouldn't even have time to sightsee. However, Diamond Head was closer to our hotel.

Arriving in the parking lot, we saw a huge sign with the name of the volcano on it, so we asked a fellow tourist to take a picture of us with it. Then we followed the path to the entrance. The whole walkway up the mountain had metal railings, and we barely fit side-by-side. My legs began to burn because the hike was very steep, with portions featuring stairs that knocked the wind out of me from pure exertion. But when we got to the top, the view took my breath away. We stood there for a while with the wind blowing in our hair, looking at Oahu from three hundred sixty degrees.

Dominic's lips met mine on the top of that beautiful volcano. We then took tons of pictures from every angle so we would have them to help us remember our trip and to share with our family. I had been texting Susan, Dom's parents, my parents, and Lori with almost every picture we'd taken so far.

ভ৹ ভ৹ ৶ও ৶ও

The rest of our trip passed much too quickly. One day, we drove to the North Shore to spend the day at the Polynesian Cultural Center, and we even stayed for the luau at the end of the day. The PCC introduced us to life from all the surrounding islands: Samoa, Fiji, Tahiti, New Zealand, Tonga, Hawaii, and Marquesas. We saw many shows with dances from the different islands. I learned how to sew a quilt square with a flowery, Hawaiian pattern in red and white. Once it was dusk, we headed off to the luau, which was preceded by a buffet dinner with foods like poi, poke, yams, fish, pork, and other island fare. After dinner, we sat down for the show. I was excited since it took all of those elements we'd learned about earlier in the day and magnified them. When it began, we were surprised by how beautiful the costumes and dancers were. Scenes from the history of each island were acted out in dance with drums and flame twirlers. We were in awe of the performances and happy to have had the experience.

Another day, we spent a few hours at Waimea Falls. We watched some professionals cliff diving over very high water falls, and it scared the crap out of me. My fear of heights wouldn't allow me to get up to the top, but it was nice to watch from afar.

Dominic dragged me to Matsumoto's Shaved Ice. He ordered the Matsumoto special with vanilla ice cream and condensed milk, and I got the banana cream with the same extras. I had to hand it to Dominic for making us go, because it tasted delicious. It was so good, in fact, that I craved one every day we were there.

We fell in love with Oahu and were very sad to leave. Knowing that we were going to see Lucia motivated us to leave, otherwise we could have stayed forever.

ৡৢৡৢ

Using all of my vacation time for this expedition, I was able to book two more weeks off. We planned on spending them with Dominic's parents. I almost regretted the decision to go directly to New York from Hawaii when we were forced to endure a six-hour flight from Oahu, a layover in Los Angeles for three hours, and then another six-hour plane ride to New York. We did get to run home during our layover since we lived so close to the airport. We exchanged some of the clothes in our suitcases and figured we could wash our dirty laundry at his parent's house. The last leg of the journey was an all-nighter, which landed us at JFK at five-thirty in the morning. I felt too old to be trying to sleep on an airplane all night, and I knew Dominic felt the same way. Exhausted was an understatement for how tired we felt.

A town car picked us up from the airport and drove us straight to Park Avenue on the Upper East Side. I had never been to New York before, but I had heard about the apartments wealthier people lived in. They weren't like any places I had seen in Los Angeles or Boston. These New York homes had doormen, concierge services, and elevator operators, and they were worth a lot of money. My jaw dropped when we first entered his parent's apartment. It consisted of ten rooms, four of which were bedrooms. Dominic had tried to warn me, but nothing could have prepared me for what we walked into. Arriving on their floor, I heard my daughter's happy, boisterous laughter. What she was doing up, I had no idea, since it was only seven in the morning. I hoped Emma and Dom weren't in over their heads with my little girl and her level of energy. I knew at times she could be a bit much, but she also had good manners and knew how to behave when necessary. I trusted she had just been excited to see us.

Dominic rang the doorbell, and Emma answered with Lucia hard on her heels. I had a feeling she wanted to knock down her grandmother to get to us, but she stood there waiting as patiently as she could, bouncing on her toes. Emma received us with tons of love, and then stepped aside so we could tackle Lucia.

"Oh, my baby. I missed you so much." I had her wrapped in a tight hug, but then pulled back to look at her. "Have you been having a good time?" I wanted to see if she was nervous or showed any signs of stress, but to my pleasant surprise she looked happy and comfortable.

"Momma, I'm having fun. Susan and Vitto took care of me on the plane, and then we visited Lori and Chris, and I stayed here while they went home. Grandma made cookies with me, and we colored and went to the park," she said before taking a deep breath. "But I'm happy you're here."

She kissed me on the lips and jumped out of my arms and into Dominic's. He knelt down just in time to catch her. Her little arms wrapped around his neck, and as they hugged, they whispered into each other's ears and giggled. My heart expanded in my chest just watching how much they loved each other. When they stood up, Dominic addressed his mother.

"Where's Dad?" he asked.

"He went to the office. But come, let's get you two to your room," she answered.

We walked through their spacious apartment. Passing through an open living room and dining room, we entered a long hallway with several closed doors. Lucia came bouncing behind us.

"Momma, wait until you see my room. It's so beautiful. I want a bed like that for our house," she rambled.

"Oh? There's a bed you like? We'll see it as soon as we put our stuff in our room," said Dominic.

"Don't get any bright ideas," I told him, recognizing the tone he'd used.

"Once you settle, I'll give you a tour of the house, okay? Come find me when you're done," said Emma.

"Thank you so much, Emma. I'm so happy to be here."

Arriving at our room, my jaw dropped again. The parts of the house I had seen already were impeccably decorated. One of the rooms we had gone through had been paneled in beautiful blonde oak, and the foyer looked to be about the size of my whole condo. But this bedroom was incredibly beautiful. Every inch was painted in a shade of pea green and one wall lined with dark oak shelving. There was a sofa to match. I would never have imagined the layout and design on my own, so I was surprised at how much I liked what I was seeing. A closet sat on the opposite wall of the pullout couch, and a big window with a wonderful view of Park Avenue sat on the other. Different, but beautiful.

I set my suitcase in the closet, not bothering to unpack yet. Exhausted, I plopped myself on the sofa. Lucia climbed on my lap and just clung for a while.

Dominic joined us while we reconnected. His strong arms wrapped around the both of us while he rested his chin on my shoulder.

"Can we go see my room now?" asked Lucia.

"Of course," said Dominic.

She walked backwards, pulling on our hands to her room.

"Close your eyes," said Lucia.

With our eyes closed, we entered the room after our little girl.

"Okay, look," she said. She couldn't contain her excitement.

Dominic smirked and shook his head. I looked at him with a confused expression, not sure what he found so funny. The room was painted a pale shade of pink—perfect for little girls. The single trundle bed was a darker shade of pink with a canopy to match. The bedding was white and offset the pink.

"You see, I want a bed like that. It's so pretty."

"We'll see what we can do, okay? I'll have to ask Grandma where she got it," said Dominic.

"Was this room always like this?" I asked.

Dominic shook his head again. "She must have done this when she found out Lucia was coming to stay."

"Wow." I was touched by the idea that Emma had gone through so much trouble for our daughter.

"Let's go take our tour, and then I think I want to sleep for a while," I suggested.

Dominic bent down and kissed me. "Whatever you want, honey."

Chapter 29
Peek-a-Boo

The weather in New York City in the summer was thick and humid. Walking around the city while surrounded by all of the tall buildings that blocked the ocean breeze, my clothes stuck to me, and I was sweating like a pig. But on the bright side, I fell in love with Manhattan. Times Square was a sight to see with so many flashing lights of all different colors coming off the buildings. Big screens everywhere showed commercials and advertisements. Street performers and people dressed as super heroes were all over the place trying to make a buck.

Even I was able to tell the difference between the locals and the tourists. The locals just walked with purpose and bumped into anyone in their way. It was kind of hilarious. The tourists, however, walked around with their heads up and eyes unfocused, looking completely dazed. The fast-paced ambiance made me feel comfortable, although I wasn't sure why. Los Angeles moved much slower, and Boston, although faster-paced than L.A., was still slower than New York.

Dominic took us to all of his favorite places, and we met up with Lori and Chris several times. Emma and Dom took us to fancy restaurants and introduced Lucia and me to all of their friends. They gushed over us and told us how proud they were to have us as part of their family. I felt so close to them, even more than I had before. I was so glad that Dominic had suggested the trip to New York and that he wanted to take us to his old stomping grounds.

Everyone had completely spoiled Lucia, and she received so many gifts from all of their friends that we had to ship some of her stuff to California. I hoped she didn't think this spoiling was going to continue once we were back home. Lucia knew how to work it, too. She used her polite manners and cute smiles to get people eating out of the palm of her hand. When we told her our time was up in New York and we had to go home, she had her first temper tantrum in years. She did not want to leave, and even said we could leave without her. Now, that stung. The two weeks I'd spent on my belated honeymoon without her had been difficult. I'd felt guilty for leaving her behind and even anxious that no one would be able to care for her like I did. But that was not the case. Susan and Vitto were great substitutes for us and cared for her so well. When they left her with Emma and Dom, her grandparents had done just as well. Lucia had fallen in love with them and wanted to stay.

I needed to go home, though. It was time, and I was ready. I loved being away and sightseeing, but I missed my bed, my things, and my home. We were all packing to leave the following morning and were going to eat in for our last meal. I left Dominic in the bedroom, walked toward the kitchen, and found Lucia speaking with Dom and Emma. I decided to stay behind the entry so she wouldn't see me.

"Grandpa, don't you love me?" Oh my God! There she was, my master manipulator.

"What? Of course I do. How could you ask such a thing, Lucia?" asked Dom.

She sighed. "I just don't want to have to miss you. Can't you and grandma move near us?"

"Come here. We love you so very much, and we'd love to spend more time with you. And more than anything we'd love to be closer to you. I think we will be looking to move soon. We spoke to your daddy about that already," he answered.

"Promise?" she asked.

"Yes, I promise," he said.

I took that as my cue to enter.

"Hi. What are you two up to?"

Lucia answered first. "Oh, nothing, Momma," she said. She was still upset with me, because she was trying to strong-arm me into staying there. It wasn't going to happen. My vacation was over, and I needed to get back to work.

Emma and Dominic walked into the kitchen together, and Lucia jumped right into her daddy's arms.

"Hey, munchkin," said Dominic.

She didn't answer but instead laid her head on his shoulder and rubbed the nape of his neck with her little fingers. He held her while I helped make dinner, and she almost fell asleep in his arms. Her clingy behavior could have been from being overtired; she'd been a busy little bee since she arrived in New York. I was betting that, when we got home, she'd rest for the entire first week, which would be a perfect way for Dominic to get caught back up with his work.

The doorbell rang, and Emma went to answer it. I smiled to myself when I heard the voices of Lori and Chris. I hadn't known they were coming, but it was a pleasant surprise.

I ran toward the door and scooped Lori into my arms.

"I'm so glad you're here," I said, smiling at Chris over Lori's shoulder.

"We couldn't let you leave without seeing us," said Lori.

"Come in; you want some wine?" I asked.

Chris walked in behind us with his arm around Emma. I loved the close relationships between Dominic and Chris and Emma. I found it adorable when the boys would hug their mother, towering over her with their tall bodies. If I had a son, I hoped to have as loving a relationship with him as Emma had with her boys. Truthfully, though, I just wanted to give Dominic a child; it didn't matter if it was a girl or boy.

We sat around the kitchen island waiting for dinner to be ready, soaking up each other's company. The past year had been wonderful. My family had become closer and had grown. Looking at the faces around me, I knew I was a lucky woman.

After a wonderful dinner and great conversation, Lori and Chris went home, and we all went to bed. Our flight was scheduled to leave early the next day, and we needed some sleep. We lay wrapped around each other; Dominic and I were too tired to move.

"This has been an incredible four weeks, but I'm so ready to go home."

"Me, too," said Dominic.

"I think I might need another vacation to recoup from this vacation," I said with a giggle.

"Tell me about it … but tomorrow. I need to sleep now. I love you," he said and kissed my head.

"Good night. Love you, too."

❧❧❧❧

Our flight was uneventful, and we arrived home tired but in one piece. Without even an ounce of energy to unpack or do anything else, I just wanted to sleep. I had to work the following day, so I had to force myself into getting things unpacked and cleaned up before I could sit for a moment. We still had to deal with the clothes we had just dumped on the bed during our layover in New York the previous week. In other words, our lives were back to normal.

For some reason, it felt like the jet lag was knocking me on my ass. We had been home for two weeks, and all I wanted to do was sleep. I'd fall asleep at my desk, at the dinner table, and as soon as my head hit the pillow at night. My body felt like it was worn out and heavy all the time. It was horrible. Dominic thought I was sick and said my exhaustion wasn't normal. He swore I had caught some sort of island disease in Hawaii, and he made me an appointment with my doctor and dragged me there. I just figured since we had been gone so long and had bounced from such extreme time zones that the travel had affected me worse this time around.

It annoyed me that I had to ask for another day off, but I was resigned to the idea. Entering the doctor's office, I became very nervous. Dominic's fears about some island disease crept up on me and freaked me out. Whatever I had, I just hoped the doctor could give me something to fix it. Dominic was in the waiting room with Lucia, and I knew he was nervous as well. He had been babying me ever since I'd begun showing signs of an illness.

The door to my room opened, and my doctor came in. "Mrs. Roberts, how are you today?" he asked.

"Hi, Doctor Park. Um, well, today I'm like I have been for the past two weeks: completely exhausted. I mean, I've been so tired, and my body has been so heavy. I can't move or stay awake," I said.

"Okay, are there any other symptoms?"

130

I had to think about it. "No, I just think crankiness, but that has to be from being so tired all the time. We just got back home two weeks ago from a month-long trip. We went to Hawaii for two weeks, and then to New York for another two weeks. I just thought it was the extreme time changes."

"Yes, that could have impacted you in some way, but I need to ask when you had your last menstrual period."

I answered instantly, without thought. "Last month on the thirteenth," I said, but that didn't seem right. No, last month, two weeks ago, we were in New York on that date, and I hadn't gotten my period in New York or Hawaii. "No, it was the month before that," I said.

"Okay, then. Pregnancy is a possibility, but I'd like to run some blood tests—not just for that, but other things as well. I'll send the nurse in to take your blood, and we'll send it to the lab. In the meantime, let's do a urine test."

I nodded. I had no idea what to say, and I didn't want to get my hopes up and then be let down. The doctor handed me a urine cup and sent me to the restroom. My head was spinning, and I couldn't keep up with all the thoughts flying through it. We had tried for almost seven months, and all it took was one vacation to make it happen.

After doing my business in the bathroom, I returned to the examination table on shaky legs. The nurse came in for the urine sample, and then returned to take my blood. She took several vials. After she'd poked my veins too many times, I knew I'd have a big bruise on my arm.

Before I left the exam room, the doctor gave me the results to the urine test. Doctor Park explained it would be best to wait for the blood test results to be sure. After all the emotional ups and downs with trying to get pregnant, I decided that would be best.

When I walked into the waiting room, I searched for Dominic immediately. My face must have scared him because, in a flash, he threw his magazine down and almost ran across the room to me. With his hands on my shoulders, he asked what the doctor had said.

"Nothing much. He took blood and said we'll get the results in a few days. It just made me nervous. Now I have to wait to find out what is wrong with me," I said.

I ended up waiting five days for a phone call from my doctor's office. The wait was painful, but I didn't want to tell Dominic it was possible I was pregnant until I was sure. I knew it would hurt him if I had to let him down in the end. But when I got the call, the results shocked the hell out of me. I couldn't wait to share the news with Dominic and Lucia—I knew they would both just jump for joy.

❧❧❧❧

After I left work the day of the phone call, I stopped at a print shop on the way home. The store was able to print my items while I waited, and I went home with my loot, very giddy.

Arriving home, I parked my car and rode the elevator to my floor. The scent of garlic wafted through the hallway, and I hoped it was coming from our condo. Slipping my key in the door, I walked in and knew instantly that Dominic had cooked linguini with clam sauce. My stomach let out a loud growl. I peeked into the kitchen and saw him at the stove.

"Hey, babe," I said.

He walked over to me and kissed hard on the lips. "Hi, honey. How was your day?" he asked.

"It was good. If that is ready, can you turn it off for a minute??" I said, pointing to the stove. I was too eager to wait until after dinner.

"Yeah, sure. Go and sit down, and I'll be right there."

"Lucia?" I called for her. She came running out of her room and jumped into my arms. I planted kisses all over her face "Hi, kiddo. Can you come and sit with us so we can talk?" I asked. She nodded and ran to the sofa.

Dominic came over and sat next to Lucia so that she was between us. The expression on his face was one of concern. I felt bad for making him worry for nothing, but I hoped the surprise would make it all better.

"I bought you two a surprise."

Dominic's eyebrows scrunched down in confusion. Lucia began bouncing in her seat.

"Okay, I'm going to give them to you, but you have to open them at the same time. Only when I say you can," I said.

They both nodded, and I handed them the little gift bags.

"Ready? Open it!" I yelled.

I sat and watched them pull the tissue paper out of their little yellow gift bags until they got to the gift at the bottom. Lucia pulled hers out first, but I didn't think she'd be able to read it without help. When my eyes flickered back to Dominic, he had the gift spread out on his lap. "Read it out loud," I said.

He held up the plain white t-shirt and read, "My wife has a bun in the oven." His face opened up to wide eyes and a big smile. "Is this for real?"

I nodded, tears streaming down my face.

"Can I read mine out loud?" asked Lucia.

"Go ahead, Lucia," I said and gestured toward her shirt.

Dominic held it up for her to see, and she said, "I'm going to be a big sister." She looked from me to Dominic and to me again. "I am?" she asked.

"Yup," I answered.

"When? I want it now!" she screeched.

Dominic and I laughed at her excitement. "Well, the doctor said the baby won't come until March twentieth of next year," I explained.

"What? Why so long? Is it a girl or boy?"

"I don't know yet. It's too soon to tell. But listen — after dinner I'll show you what the baby looks like now on the computer. Okay?"

"Yes! Okay, let's eat." She jumped up and ran to the table.

Dominic pulled me to him and engulfed me in his arms.

"I'm so happy. I didn't think it was possible to feel happier than I did when I met you, but I was wrong. How can I even begin to express how much more my heart is swelling to fit all the love and happiness I feel for you, Lucia, and now our new baby? I love you. Thank you for loving me and making all my dreams come true," he said while his voice cracked from his overwhelming emotion.

"Please don't ever thank me for loving you. Loving you and being with you and now expanding our family with you makes me the happiest person on the planet. I love you with all my heart," I said.

The End

ABOUT THE AUTHOR

Jennifer Garcia's lifelong love for reading and writing was put aside for many years while she made her way in the world and nurtured her young family. Originally from Boston, she currently resides in Los Angeles with her husband, two sons, and two dogs. She'll give you the sweetest romance to tempt your sweet tooth.

Keep up to date with all my new releases and writing info on my blog: jenniferfgarcia.com

Here's a sneak peek of my novella, *In My Mother's Footsteps.*

Summary:

Anela Alborn's life is a lie. After growing up without the love of a father, her mother reveals his identity. Tragedy strikes and she sets off on an adventure that leads to more than she could ever imagine. Bumping into Christian Sivers distracts her from the real man of her dreams, her father. Will he live up to her dreams? And does she follow in her mother's footsteps?

Chapter 1

Knowledge

"Anela," Lennie Metting, our family attorney and longtime family friend, said as he tried to get my attention. "Anela, I need to know that you understand what I've read to you. Go through those papers soon; your graduation gift is in there as well. She left it with me, not knowing if you'd want to see her, but she wanted you to have it." I nodded in reply.

Lennie and I were sitting in comfortable, dark brown, leather chairs next to the window in his office. The space was made up of sleek lines and cold metals that looked as solemn as I felt. The beautiful view of the ocean with Angel Island in the distance spilled in through the grand window, contrasting with both the décor and my mood. While tears streamed down my face, the beauty was lost on me. I sat in a complete daze and tried to process what the man sitting across from me had said.

"Would you like some water?" he asked. Shaking my head, I looked up and met his steel-gray eyes. They were kind and sympathetic. The recent death pained him, too. The beard on his face compensated for the lack of hair on the top of his head. His short stature did not reflect his character, for he was a fierce and passionate man. In court, Lennie's reputation preceded him, but no one saw the kind man that my mother and I knew.

"No, thank you. I'm fine. Um . . . so is that all?" I tapped the file he'd given me after his speech.

"Yes, but I want you to call me if you need anything — and I do mean *anything*. You hear?" He started to stand.

I'd noticed how uncomfortable he appeared to be during the meeting, but he'd been very helpful nonetheless. In the last few weeks, he had assisted me in making the funeral arrangements and dealing with all of the legal paperwork that fell onto my shoulders.

Rising, I stuck out my hand for a formal shake, but instead Lennie pulled me into an embrace.

"Anela, please take care of yourself. Your mother would be very disappointed in me if I let anything happen to you, okay? And call me if you need anything."

"I understand, and thank you, Lennie." Pulling myself from his arms took a great deal of strength. I longed for the feeling of a father's love and wanted to hold on to it for as long as I could, but I had to go. My mind needed sorting, and there were plans to make.

As I made my way out of the office and back to my small cottage in Sausalito, California, I felt the panic come on. The list of things that I needed to do was mounting and I felt overwhelmed.

❦❦❦❦❦

Upon opening the door to the home I had shared with my mother since my birth, her scent hit me, just like it had every time I walked in here over the past two weeks. I wandered without cause around the small cottage before I plopped myself down on the couch. Everything in that house was old and artsy, just like the little town she lived in. My mother, Carla, had been an artist — a hippy, even — and had fit so well with the other residents of Sausalito.

At twenty-two years old, I was about to graduate from Berkeley University in a week with a bachelor's degree in business management — for lack of a passion for anything else. My graduation had been something my mother had been looking forward to seeing, but she would never get to now. I'd been in my dorm room, studying for finals, when I received the phone call that my mother had passed away in our family home. She'd never been sick, so it hadn't made sense until the results of the autopsy were revealed. The coroner had concluded that Carla had had an aneurism that burst and drowned her brain. Research taught me what an aneurism was, and I found out that she must have been suffering from headaches and hadn't told anyone. Or maybe she *had* told someone; it just wasn't me. I hadn't been speaking to her at the time, after all.

It had always been just the two of us, since we didn't have any other family left. She had a few friends around town, but none that I knew very well. With a shake of my head, I turned my attention to the list of things I needed to get done.

First thing on the list: I had to pack up my mother's belongings. The nagging urge to go through her stuff and find something sentimental kept bothering me. I needed to find a connection with my mother, even if I was angry with her. She'd left me all alone, and I was livid about the lie I had been led to believe my whole life.

When I was about to start my senior year of college, Carla had sprung some life-changing and surprising news on me.

I'd come home for the summer and everything had been great. I indulged my love for running often, but it was a solitary thing, mainly because my mother refused to go with me. She always laughed that she was much too old and out of shape to start running. So instead, I ran in the mornings while it was still brisk, and in exchange, I'd let her teach me how to paint. In all honesty, I had zero talent and painted like a five year old, but she loved everything I'd created and told me she'd always cherish them.

During one of our sessions, I watched her paint the most beautiful scenery: a small chapel on the beach surrounded by billowing palm trees and lush plumeria trees. The colorful stained glass windows of the chapel reflected the sun and shot rays across the sand. When I asked her about it, she said it was her favorite place in the world. The whole scene blew me away, and I felt myself being absorbed by its inviting nature. But when I asked her where it was, she replied with a single word: Ko'Olina. That had been all she gave me. I shrugged it off and didn't think too much about it.

Right before I left to head back to school, she sat me down — very formally — and began to tell me a tale.

"Darling, listen to me. I have to tell you this before it kills me," she said with a blank face. She showed no emotion at all. It was like she had practiced it a million times, all so she could get through it without breaking down. "I know I told you that you didn't have a father and that he was dead. But I lied."

Her hands were working, steady and strong, to fold and unfold the pleat on her skirt.

"After I graduated high school, I took a vacation to Oahu, Hawaii. I spent a month there with my friends, just exploring the island and enjoying myself." While she spoke, she didn't look at me. Instead, she watched her hands work on her skirt. "It was a gift from my parents. They were old and didn't have the strength to take me anywhere themselves, so they sent me there with my two best friends at the time. Well, anyway, I met this soldier. He pursued me, and things just happened. We spent a lot of time together, and I ditched my friends, which they never forgave me for," she said, looking up at me for a moment.

"On my last night, we made love. He gave me his address, and I went home, never looking back. Then, I found out I was pregnant with you."

Still looking her in the eye, I could see her plea for understanding, but I couldn't give it to her, because I still didn't understand.

My heart began to beat in fury as if it had figured out the story before I did. I looked at my mother in such great confusion, knowing my eyes were pleading for a better explanation. Bitterness lodged itself inside me because the last thing I had allowed my mother to say to me had my world crashing down on me.

As my mother sat there telling me the tale of how she met her soldier and how I came to be, I couldn't believe my ears.

"So, he didn't die in battle somewhere? I mean, you told me my father died before he could even meet me!"

"No, angel, he's very much alive. At least the last time I checked, he was."

Sitting there unable to move and listening in disbelief, my mouth had hung open in surprise and fury at her gall. I could not believe the words that were coming out of her mouth. It was all too much. My mother knew how much I had longed for a father, yet she'd failed to tell me I had one out there. How dared she?

Tingles swept through my body, and I began to sway. My ears plugged, and when I closed my eyes to steady myself, I saw stars. I could sense the signs of a faint coming on, so I plopped myself back in the chair like a sack of potatoes, feeling defeated. Scooting my seat back, I shoved my head between my knees, most of all because I wanted to hide my face from my mother.

Then she spoke again.

"Anela, listen to me. I did what I thought was best. We had two different lives. I didn't want to be an Army wife, and he wouldn't have left the military. He loved his job; it was his career. You know how old-fashioned Grandma and Grandpa were. They would have made me marry him. I didn't want that, so I refused to tell them. It just seemed easier."

I cut her off before she could say anything else. "Easier? Damn it, Mom. I would have had a father, for Christ's sake. Are you kidding me?"

The anger had built up and was ready to boil over.

"Anela, stop it! Things were more complicated back then. I shouldn't have even been with him before marriage, and then I showed up from vacation pregnant by a man who had promised me nothing. He had plans for a career in the Army. I didn't want to ruin that for him. Once I made my decision, I stuck with it. And that was that. I'm sorry if you don't understand, but that's the way it is," she said.

I just stared at her in disbelief, shocked at all of the selfish words pouring out of her mouth.

"Look, darling, I'm sorry. I love you so much, and I'm glad that I have you in my life." The tears rolled down her face, soaking her shirt.

I stood up in a flash and left.

After that day, I ignored her phone calls, and I never spoke to her again. I was consumed with bitterness over what she had denied me. I thought she was the most selfish person I had ever known. Her sudden and unexpected death left me with such guilt and shame. I had shunned my mother for doing what she thought was best, and it had cost me the last year of her life. My anger had made me a jerk and a spoiled brat. I hadn't deserved her love.